MY LADY EVIL

A NOVEL BY

PARLEY J. COOPER

SIMON AND SCHUSTER

NEW YORK

For four friends—
Keith Andre,
Robert Barufaldi,
Freya Manston
and
Robert Lewis

PROLOGUE

The man was found floating in the Thames clutching a black journal to his body in a frozen death grip, seemingly bent on carrying the horror of his entries with him into the sea.

It was not until the journal of André Laurent was restored that light was shed on the terrifying story of Lady Nina Hargrave. . . .

THE JOURNAL OF
ANDRE LAURENT

PART ONE

I was awakened from a fitful sleep. Exhaustion from the long trip weighed heavily upon me, and waking so abruptly, I suffered from disorientation.

Where was I?

And why was I so cold?

The names of Charles Arledge and Lady Nina Hargrave flashed through my mind. A chill, which had nothing to do with the low temperature inside the coach, ran along my spine, and the reality of my situation struck me. I had formed a liaison with Charles Arledge. I was en route to a small village where I would meet and destroy his sister. The victim, innocent of the fate that awaited her, had oddly chosen this corner of France as a retreat, a harbor in which to sit out her grief over the death of her husband and mother, one accident following the other within a two-month span.

Sighing, I pulled the heavy fur lap robe firmly about my legs, turned my face into the leather of the seat and attempted to return to sleep.

When we arrived in the village, I was in a state of half-sleeping and half-waking, a netherworld of jumbled fantasies and realities. It was to this that I attributed my first impressions of the sights that greeted me through the coach window.

Despite the downpour and the late hour, the streets were active. If it had not been for the lack of music and laughter, I would have sworn myself still in Paris, riding home through the crowds of the Left Bank. Our path was continually slowed or blocked, and the horses, now accustomed to the freedom of the open road, whined nervously and threatened to bolt. The coachman, his whip snapping angrily above the heads of the horses, was given to frequent outbursts of cursing.

Lowering the window, I stuck my head into the rain and inquired of the trouble.

"Lock your door, Monsieur," he warned. "And keep safely out of view of the window."

I stubbornly did not comply.

The crowds in the streets were not late merrymakers, as I had first suspected. They were a miserable lot, mostly dressed in rags or wrapped in tattered blankets. The doorways and awnings of the bordering buildings were a hive of activity. Men and women and children fought and shoved one another for a dry space into which to wedge their miserable bodies. I noted that many of them were on crutches, several missing limbs, a sight not uncommon since the war. Although they glanced at our passing coach, it was with a curious indifference. They were not beggars these. The coachman's concern, I realized, was due to finding himself suddenly surrounded by a phenomenal number of such unsavory citizens. Assuming they were the wanderers, the unfortunates who follow every war, I raised my window and put them from my mind.

Or attempted to do so.

Even as I prepared myself for my arrival, I could not erase the general aura of those people. They reminded me of paintings I had seen of souls waiting for admittance into hell.

At the inn, a small gratuity placed in the swollen hands of the proprietor produced a sudden vacancy of rooms facing the bell tower, the gardens and the apartment to be occupied by Lady Hargrave. The entire wing was now dark, framed by the darker blackness of the horizon which I knew to be the Mediterranean. Having declined the offer of food and drink, I retired directly and managed to unpack with the aid of a young valet named Emile.

Emile Favière is a remarkably handsome youth, with finely chiseled features and a smooth, flawless complexion. He is taller than I, with piercing eyes that hint of worldliness and a body that would lead most women and many men to disregard his position of servitude. He is too young to have been in the army, but I could not help but think what a striking figure he would have cut in uniform. Ah, but how many like Emile have I seen die or lose their youth in a single battle?

Perhaps I might make use of the handsome Emile during this campaign of evil!

There is a man in the village who claims to be a messiah. He is, Emile tells me, of Russian decent. Driven from his own country, he has collected hundreds of mesmerized followers on his trek across Europe. The sudden influx of

15

the crippled and dying—for he claims to be a healer of men—has become this community's first major problem since Napoleon's defeat and the return of the soldiers. The townspeople refer to him as a devil and have threatened to have him arrested.

But saint or devil, he has collected a large following. In addition to their unsightliness, these unfortunates bring disease which spreads unchecked.

But not all of this man's followers are poor. I have seen the enviously wealthy who reside at this inn, looking sallow and dissipated, wheeled about the lobby by uniformed nurses and muscular attendants who undoubtedly serve double purposes.

The poor continue to huddle against the sides of buildings and in doorways until they are driven away. They die of their diseases and of exposure to the elements while they wait and hope to be cured.

Last night, after unpacking, I could not sleep despite my exhaustion. Leaning against the window frame and gazing beyond the courtyard, I saw the death carts pass. One stopped directly across from the inn. Two men with masks tied about their lower faces climbed down and hoisted a body into the cart. They did not examine it, but only assumed it to be without life.

I am an atheist. Having such blind faith in a mere man, this self-claimed messiah, is beyond my comprehension. I believe only in myself and in the sensual pleasures of the flesh.

Lady Hargrave arrived in the late afternoon.

Heavily veiled, she slid from her coach and, turning neither to the left nor the right, proceeded directly through the lobby and to her rooms, leaving a bony serving creature to struggle with the register and luggage.

Lady Hargrave has remained in her rooms since her arrival.

As arranged, I have a perfect view of her windows—but the draperies were immediately drawn.

I do not expect to see Lady Hargrave until this foul weather has made a change for the better.

There is nothing to do except wait.

Once when I questioned Charles Arledge about his sister, he became extremely quiet, pensive. His face went through a complete transformation, my question having destroyed his gay, foolhardy humor of the moment. He sat staring at me with half-sight, remembering, I supposed, some aspect of his sister's personality.

Intrigued, I questioned him further.

"Is she comely?" I pressed.

"She has the face of an angel," he answered.

There was an intonation in his voice that had silenced all further questions.

The rain continues.

Confined to my rooms and unable to begin my conquest

of Lady Hargrave, I stare at the white pages of this journal and much of my past returns to haunt me.

I have never been a happy man. My unhappiness I attribute to constantly reaching for that which is beyond my grasp. As a child, I wasted my youth wishing for maturity. Once mature, I regretted the loss of my youth. Such has been the vicious cycle of my life.

But it is not the time for personal remembrances.

My mind should be occupied by this present scheme.

I am a victim of circumstance.

I had no choice but to accept Charles Arledge's proposal despite my hesitations and personal moral viewpoint. I hope, however, he does not do me the injustice of believing I accept our liaison, as he indicated, to be a spur-of-the-moment decision. I am not an educated man—I did not attend Oxford or any other institute of higher learning —but life itself has taught me much. I know the murder of his sister is a well-conceived plan over which he has labored to the most minute detail.

Of his circle of friends, only I never had the honor of meeting his family—an affront that often gave me sleepless nights. Perhaps, I told myself, he did not feel me capable of carrying off the charade of respectability, but properly instructed, I would have been as presentable as any of the dandies and fay boys of his acquaintance. Now, of course, I understand my exclusion from weekends at his family's Yarmouth estate. His plan for me was formulating even at the beginning of our acquaintance.

More important, and something I have only recently come to realize, is that the scandal from which Charles so gallantly rescued me was prearranged. Such an action guaranteed my unwaivering gratitude.

Well, my gratitude—and the threat of his dredging up damning evidence against me—does assure him of my assistance.

I will turn my attention to the project at hand—and accept my fate.

The widowed Lady Hargrave remains within her rooms.

This evening as I stood staring down into the rain-drenched courtyard, my eyes caught a fluttering movement of the draperies of Lady Hargrave's window. I shifted my gaze and had a fleeting glimpse of her face. She must have also seen me because she let the draperies fall quickly closed.

If only this intolerable weather would make a change for the better.

Lady Hargrave wore a gown and veil of black. The veil, pushed back over her hair, framed her pale, almost color-less face. She wore no jewelry and did not allow herself the customary handkerchief of acceptable white lace; it too was black, tucked into her cuff. As she paced about the garden, I noted that the only splash of color attached to her was the small book she carried. She clutched it to her bosom, a book bound in blood red, and I found myself, because of it, chillingly equating her with the deadly black widow spider.

The thought kept me momentarily in the doorway of the inn.

The rain had stopped during breakfast and the sun, although weak, had driven away some of the gloom attached to the inn. The guests, acting like animals suddenly released into the wilds, had mostly departed for a day of sight-seeing and buying. A calm had settled over the inn; even the proprietor, a man with a nervous disposition, dozed in his cage.

I watched Lady Hargrave as she paced the walkways of the garden. She settled on a concrete bench and sat for a moment with her head back to expose her face to the warmth of the sun. There was much about her that reminded me of her brother. Both had delicate features and the same aristocratic nose that gave the illusion of turning upward at the tip. Even though I could not see them at my distance, I knew her eyes would be as blue and unfathomable as those of Charles.

I clung indecisively to the doorway. Knowing I must go forward and strike up an acquaintance set my legs to shaking. I leaned into the frame and tried to concentrate on the financial rewards ahead of me. When this did nothing to quiet my shaking, I thought of what Charles would do to me should I fail him.

I stepped into the garden with renewed determination. Hoping I seemed a guest out for an innocent breath of air, I approached her bench slowly.

When she became aware that she was not alone, she glanced up. Our eyes met, and I was immediately taken aback by her expression. Her eyes were as blue and as cold as I've seen. There was no innocence, no shyness reflected in her gaze. I felt as though she saw into the very core of my being. I remembered my reaction when Charles had spoken of his sister's face as that of an angel, and that same unexplainable sense of foreboding seized me.

Even more shaken now, I sank quickly to the bench beside her before my legs could develop a will of their own and carry me hastily back to the inn. My movement was too quick, it seemed, for she moved suddenly and made as if to rise.

"It's always nicest after a storm," I managed. "The air is fresher."

She did not speak, but merely continued to sit and stare at me. One of the pins holding back her veil had slipped free of her hair, and the black lace had fallen to conceal half her face.

"I think it will rain again before nightfall," I said, hoping this would not be an accurate prediction. I had no desire to be cooped up once again in my rooms.

She set her book on the bench between us. I had the distinct feeling she had attached some unimaginable importance to it; that she considered it a barrier between us. Still, she did not speak.

I sighed and stretched my legs. "It must be pleasant here in the spring," I said. "Winter and summer always dull the natural colors."

She remained silent for an agonizing moment before saying, "I enjoy all four of the seasons. I think anyone who doesn't is a fool."

Her voice was low-pitched and enveloping. Yet here too, there was no sign of the expected demure lady of her class. Her words had been meant to criticize me, to drive me away so that she could regain her peace with the garden.

"You are right, of course," I said agreeably.

She smiled. "Am I? Then on second examination, you find winter as much to your liking as summer?" She was mocking me.

What was I to answer? I wasn't prepared to lie about my feelings toward the weather. Actually, I hated winter. It is a season meant only for the rich, who can use it as an excuse to travel to various resorts.

"I have a slight affliction," I lied. "Weather, cold weather, affects me physically."

"You seem rather young for a rheumatic condition," she remarked. "My father claims a similar ailment, but only when he is attempting to fill a conversational lag."

My face flushed, and I looked away. *Damn her,* I thought.

When I turned back to her, she was gazing off in the direction of the harbor. There were two ships in port, both flying French flags. Their reflections were cast across the shimmering surface of the water.

"You wear a mourning gown," I said as if only then aware of her attire. "Is it for your husband?"

Her voice displayed no particular emotion—certainly no tone of grief—as she answered, "My mother and my husband."

"I understand your grief. My beloved sister died but a short time ago. We were very close. I have never fully reconciled myself to the loss," I lied. I never had a sister, but the idea intrigued me. "Actually," I said, "it was because of my sister that I was compelled to approach you."

She turned and looked at me directly. Again those cold blue eyes probed mine. Her lips quivered slightly, and for one brief moment I feared she would break into laughter, having read the label of FAKE within my soul.

I affected a piteous expression. Still, I could not hold her gaze. A chambermaid saved me by crossing noisily from the inn to the back gate with a night pail in each hand. If she had not afforded me an excuse to look away from Lady Hargrave, I am certain my charade would have been finished before it had really begun.

"Are you going to explain yourself?" she asked.

Relaxing, I turned back to her. "Some quality about you reminds me of my late sister," I told her. "Oh, it's nothing definite. Perhaps the manner in which you move or tilt your head slightly. Maybe it's the way you seem to make yourself a part of the garden." I lowered my eyes for an instant, drew strength for my performance and then added, "I wonder if grief over the loss of a loved one ever subsides?"

Lady Hargrave turned her attention back to the harbor. "Isn't it strange," she asked quietly, "how easily people present their grief to strangers?"

There was a hint of malice in her tone. Again I damned her. *She will pay!*

"Forgive me," I begged. "I did not mean to burden you." I hoped I had conveyed the proper mixture of apology and indignation at her rebuke.

"Grief is so easily shared," she said. "Isn't it a pity that joy cannot equally be so?"

I thought her statement odd. A person stricken by grief

does not normally consider the limitations of joy.

"Perhaps," I offered, "it is because joy is so much more precious that we tend to guard it selfishly."

"Perhaps," she agreed thoughtfully. "Your perception is keen, Monsieur."

One of the fastenings on the back of her gown had slipped its hook. When her body expanded with her breathing, the material parted to reveal a glimpse of her undergarments. I felt suddenly as if I had stolen a moment of intimacy.

She stiffened suddenly as if affected by my vibrations. Then she took the book from the bench between us, opened it and buried her attention among the pages. That, I saw, was the book's significance: it was the device by which I was to be dismissed. She had grown bored with me. Our short interview was at an end.

Rising awkwardly, I bowed slightly and, turning on my heels, made for the open door of the inn. The proprietor had roused himself and was sweeping the stoop. He smiled and bade me a good morning.

I ignored him.

The storm reversed itself and struck a second time with even greater fury. The streets have became rivers of mud, and even the death carts are forced to discontinue their nightly rounds. The dispositions of the inn's guests match the weather.

Lady Hargrave's draperies remain drawn.

There has been a murder in the town—a teen-age girl whose mutilated body was discovered beside the highway. The conversation at the inn is limited to nothing else. The girl, it is said, had her heart carved from her chest, her eyes gouged from their sockets. An upside-down cross had been carved over the soft flesh of her abdomen. The servants talk of witchcraft, but I have no time to listen to their fears.

Despite the fires that blazed at either end of the dining room, the air was damp, uncomfortable. The guests were subdued, as dreary as the weather. Unlike myself, they appeared to have dressed hurriedly, wearing the least expensive items in their wardrobes and saving their best attire for some future occasion when the sun might choose to shine. My trousers and coats, of course, are all new— purchased at Charles's expense. It is important that my impression on Lady Hargrave be a good one. I spend a great deal of time before my mirror inspecting each detail of my appearance before descending to each meal.

Lunch today found Lady Hargrave at the table beside mine. I believe the proprietor suspects a romantic conquest and is doing his part for Cupid. Lady Hargrave, sitting in the same position I had chosen, with her back to the cherub-painted walls, was visible to me only in profile. She had not changed her black mourning gown, but she carried several news sheets instead of her red book. Most of the gentlemen and ladies were watching her—some boldly and others with discretion. Isn't it strange how the rich like to study their own?

We had completed our main course and had started our dessert and espresso before I had worked up enough courage to venture speaking.

"I believe the proprietor is afraid we will cancel our stay," I said. "He has arranged for some local actors to entertain us this evening."

She had previously decided, I felt, not to speak to me should I be so forward as to open a second conversation, but since several nearby guests had turned to listen, she could not totally ignore me without being considered a foreign snob. The English, after all, are still looked upon with considerable hostility.

Lady Hargrave gave me a lingering glance, folded her napkin and inclined her head slightly in my direction. "I am not an admirer of the theater," she announced coolly.

"But surely any diversion would be welcomed under the circumstances," I persisted. "Surely you will attend."

"I have a previous engagement, Monsieur." Draining the last of her espresso, she rose, nodded to me, then defiantly to the other guests. She swept from the dining room with the carriage of a queen.

After Lady Hargrave had made her exit, the guests went back to the serious business of dining. I offered them no fascination.

Lady Hargrave left the inn immediately following dinner. Although the pathetic efforts of the local actors had long since been finished, she had not returned.

I lingered about the lobby until my eyes were about to close of their own accord. The proprietor was watching me with amusement. Although his relief had arrived, he continued to hang about behind the desk, shuffling through mounds of papers and pretending occupation.

When I finally decided to retire, I spotted the coachman who had driven Lady Hargrave away from the inn earlier that evening. He was preoccupied with his drenched coat, shaking the rain onto the carpet, and did not notice me as I approached.

"Were you the coachman for Lady Hargrave?" I asked of him.

"I was." The tone of his voice expressed irritation.

"A bad night for traveling about," I sympathized. "Her appointment must have been extremely urgent."

" 'Urgent,' " he echoed. " 'Foolish' would be a better description." He brushed the rain from his brow with the palm of a wrinkled hand. The proprietor had spotted him and was rushing from behind his desk to rescue his endangered carpet.

I forced a laugh and said quickly, "Women are never detained by weather when it is a rendezvous with a handsome lover."

He glanced at me suspiciously, aware that I was interrogating him about his passenger's journey. His expression, however, softened when, as had the proprietor, he decided I was smitten by the noble Englishwoman. "There was no handsome lover," he informed me, and laughed good-humoredly when he saw my relief. "You can relax, my man," he said. "Your lady went to visit the mystic."

"The mystic?"

"Aye, the mystic," he repeated. "That devil that some call a messiah." His brows suddenly came together as he peered at me intently. "If I should be taken by a lady, I should concern myself more over such a visit than over the possibility of a romantic rival. It is easier to compete with a rival for affection. But this man . . . ah, he is another matter entirely, Monsieur. He is after not only the heart, but the soul as well." He stopped talking and stood clucking senselessly beneath his breath.

While the coachman was scurried away toward the kitchen by a complaining proprietor, I stood staring down at the water spots on the carpet trying to unravel the mystery of Lady Nina Hargrave.

Why should she be compelled to pay a visit to the mystic?

And why had she not returned with the coachman?

It is late.

I have tried to sleep, but I cannot.

I am remembering my wife. I suppose I should attempt to capture her on paper. It was, after all, because of Jacqueline that I came to meet Charles Arledge and become enmeshed in his plot to murder his sister.

I will say nothing of my meeting with Jacqueline except that fate dealt me an ironic blow.

We—Jacqueline and I—had both been charading as

wealthy Parisians with the intent of making good matches. As our luck would have it, we met each other instead and did not learn of our mistakes until the contracts had been signed.

When we discovered the irony of our union, we took it in completely different fashions. Jacqueline, being naturally capricious by nature, turned to love affairs, while I, developing a passion for her, attempted to walk a straight and narrow path. Jacqueline was, I reasoned, alluring and desirable, and since I found myself married to her, I gave my feelings toward her the romantic interpretation of love, although, in truth, they fell short even of infatuation.

Jacqueline's feelings toward me were quite different. She would not accept the fact that we had both played the marriage game and lost. She took my poverty as a personal affront. I had duped her and she resented me for it. The fact that her trickery equaled mine played no part in her evaluation. I had to be punished. She was not about to be held back by one marriage failure. If she could not marry a wealthy man, she told me, she would become the mistress of one. She set about to find a man of means, and at the same time to give me what she decided I deserved.

My just desert, according to Jacqueline, was emasculation. To this date I do not know how she succeeded in making me feel inferior in my masculinity, but she did succeed.

One turn of events she had not counted on, however, was my obsession with her. The more she degraded me the more fervently I felt I needed her, desired her.

Because I thought myself inferior, I accepted her many

affairs—mostly, I suppose, because they never lasted more than a few torturous days. She was not the loving woman she imagined. I always understood her affairs would end and she would come creeping back into my bed. I reasoned that she could give her body to other men, but her love would eventually be given only to me.

How foolish I was as a young man.

I should have understood that it was impossible to outlive her hatred. Women do not live long without love. It is as essential to them as food and drink. Even if it exists only in their minds, it must exist to make them feel alive. Still hating me, Jacqueline found an Englishman to lavish with her affections, a representative sent by his country for the first and last attempt at a peace conference. She met him at a friend's salon, and spoke about him openly.

I did not feel threatened by him until I noticed that her entourage of admirers had considerably dwindled. Then I became more than a little concerned and began to watch her more closely. Her cheeks were continually flushed, and her eyes sparkled with an excitement I had never seen in her before. Nothing renders a woman more agreeable than love. And Jacqueline, even Jacqueline, became agreeable.

Deciding to play detective, I took to missing my work, to hiding in doorways across from our flat in hopes of following her to one of her rendezvous. I had no idea what my actions would be once I caught her with the Englishman, but I had already considered killing him. I had, in truth, dreamed of nothing else.

Several days later, I discovered a tearful Jacqueline in her boudoir. The peace conference had been a failure, and her Englishman was returning to London. I felt relief, but only for an instant. Her lover was, she informed me, making arrangements to send for her. She would leave me when the arrangements had been completed, and she hoped I would rot in the squalor to which I had brought her. She divided the fault for her separation from her lover among the war, Napoleon himself and me. I, of course, received the greatest share of blame.

The following morning I withdrew my savings, meager as they were, from their hiding place. I purchased a pistol and waited for the first letter to arrive from her Englishman. As soon as I had his address, I intended to somehow reach London and to have retribution by murdering him.

Ah, yes. Youth is a time for foolishness, a time for passion and dramatics.

Now as a mature man, I oddly think of this and have the vague, disturbing sensation of having lost something of value.

My eyes grow heavy and I think I might sleep at last. I will write more of London, of Jacqueline's Englishman and of my meeting with Charles Arledge at a later date.

Tomorrow I will visit the mystic.

His name is Aleksandre Denisov.

He is an awe-inspiring man, with eyes that have seen other worlds. He is bearded, and his beard is unkempt, streaked with reds and grays and his natural black coloring. His neck is long and powerful. Although he wears a robe of coarse gray wool, it does not conceal his lithe, muscular frame. I was struck by the realization that he had the appearance of the Christ in a painting I once glimpsed in a Paris museum.

When I entered his hovel, he was seated at a long, crudely constructed table. There were papers spread about him, some of which had fallen to the floor and lay unretrieved. Pen in hand, he was gazing through the paneless window. He must have seen my coach arrive, but he had made no effort to rise and greet me.

I stood for a moment without speaking, expecting him to acknowledge my presence. When he did not, I introduced myself.

"My name is André Laurent."

He raised his hand to silence me. Then, bending over his papers, he began to write with fervor.

I took the liberty of the only remaining chair and sat watching him. Since the table was cluttered with papers, I crossed my legs and placed my hat on my knee.

The one-room farmhouse that he had adopted as his quarters was no more than an abandoned ruin. Aside from the two chairs that we occupied and the table, the only other item of furnishing was a plank of pine with short legs and straw on top. I assumed he used this as his bed. There was a blanket neatly folded on the hearth, and an unclean plate stood on the mantel. Even with the chill in the air, the fire had been laid but not lighted. The dust, it seemed, was more in possession of the room than the man who sat before me.

I tried to imagine Lady Hargrave in these surroundings, but I could not. I rejected the image of her black mourning gown collecting the dust from the floor. But it was because of Lady Hargrave that I had come. I was seeking information that might be used to my advantage. She had visited this man last night, and I was certain there were things he could tell me that might prove invaluable.

I turned my attention back to the farmhouse to smother my impatience. It stood on a slight rise of land. Beyond the open door, the sloping terrain was spotted by those followers of Denisov who were waiting for him to make his morning appearance. The village lay on the horizon, the steeples and housetops framed against the blue of the bay of Marseille beyond.

I stared at Denisov.

The man filled me with a strange apprehension. I have never been at ease with those who embrace religion—any religion—with dedication. I had found it difficult enough to abide their aura of salvation when they were attired in the fashion of the day, but Denisov, still ignoring me, clad in his Christ-like robe with his naked feet protruding from beneath the hem, was an even greater source of exasperation.

He suddenly laid his pen aside and, leaning back in his chair, stared at me from across the cluttered table. I felt a mysterious power in his gaze, and this upset me all the more.

"My name is André Laurent," I repeated. "People at the inn where I am staying have talked about you, and I felt a need to see you for myself."

He continued to stare at me, his eyes, I noted, seldom

blinking. He had folded his hands on top of his papers, and I noticed that the ink had been smeared across his long, slender fingers. His eyes probed mine, and I felt a queasiness in the pit of my stomach.

"I am at a loss to explain my compulsion to see you," I went on, attempting to shrug away my nervousness with a senseless laugh.

Denisov shifted his weight to his elbows without moving his hands. When he spoke, it was in a calm, deep-throated voice. "You are not the usual sort who is drawn to me. Are you a Christian, Monsieur Laurent?"

I had not anticipated his questioning my belief. He was rumored to consider himself a messiah. I had come to him. Was that not enough? I uncrossed my legs and awkwardly lost my hat to the dust of the floor. When I straightened from retrieving it, he had not altered his position or expression.

"Do you, indeed, believe in anything beyond the reality of yourself?"

I said nothing.

"I thought not," he finally said wearily. "Devotion outside oneself seems to have been abandoned primarily to the afflicted."

Rising suddenly and clasping his hands behind his back, Denisov began to pace about the room. His shoulders were stooped as if he were laden with a heavy burden. "It is true that people talk of me," he said. "But what are they saying?" He turned to face me, and his dark eyes bored into mine.

I could not hold his gaze.

"They whisper that I am a messiah," he went on. More

bitterly, he added, "A messiah! Not *the* Messiah! And a messiah of what? From where? Heaven?" His voice became lower as he added, "Or Hell?"

When my head snapped up, I saw that he had turned away from me and was pacing toward the paneless window. His shoulders were now straight, his hands clasped together so tightly that I could see the whitening of his knuckles.

"People are saying that I bring discord wherever I go," he said. "That I create ripples in the calm streams of their lives. Now that the war is ended, they want only pleasant things to occupy their minds. It is a difficult time for me. Never have so many been so ripe for what I teach, but still they reject me."

"Are you harassed?" I asked.

"Harassed? No. The masses do not believe in me openly, but neither do they completely reject me. It is safer, you see?" He glanced at me over his shoulder. "If I am from Hell, they would be forced to face themselves. Ah, but if I am from Heaven, rejection of me might mean the closing of that particular door." He paused at the window and, leaning on the sill, gazed out at the crowds of his unfortunate followers who had began to gather on the slope. "Even they demand miracles," he said with a heavy sigh. "Nothing less than miracles will satisfy them."

"Not being a Christian myself, I can understand that," I told him. "Life commands us to adjust to reality, and yet religion is based on the acceptance of pure fantasy."

He looked at me again over his shoulder, and there was a new expression on his face that I could not interpret. "Perhaps there is hope for you yet, Monsieur Laurent."

35

I did not ask for an explanation of his statement. I wanted no sermons. I had come for another purpose entirely.

"There can be a communion of the two, of reality and fantasy," he said softly. "There is such a fine line between them—as there is between varying . . . religions."

"There can be a communion of the two if that fine line is bridged by miracles," I mumbled. "If you could perform miracles as it is rumored that Jesus . . ." I let my statement trail off incomplete.

Denisov came away from the window and returned to his chair behind the table. "You have already determined which kingdom I represent," he said, and smiled, revealing even, white teeth. His smile faded quickly. "But you did not come to prove my authenticity in either case, Monsieur Laurent. What is it that has brought you? Do you wish to donate your wealth to our cause, so that you might guarantee your immortality in the event religion is not pure fantasy?" He made little effort to conceal his opinion of me.

"My wealth would be of little consequence," I told him truthfully. "I came for information."

"What information?"

"You have had a certain visitor," I said. "A young Englishwoman who has recently lost her husband and mother and is staying at the inn during her period of mourning."

He nodded, remembering.

"Lady Hargrave's welfare is my chief concern," I lied. "Her grief is genuine, but I do not know its depth. I fear she might cause herself harm during her adjustment to her losses."

"Yes, I remember the lady," Denisov told me. He bent back over his papers, but not before I noted yet another indiscernible change of expression.

"She finds it difficult to converse with me," I said. "I was hopeful that you might share your conversations with me so that I might be of greater aid to her during these dark moments."

"Are you her suitor, Monsieur?" he asked with interest.

"No, a close friend of the family."

"Hers, or her husband's?"

"Hers."

"I see." He was silent for several moments, sitting quietly and staring into my eyes. Finally, he rose again and stood towering above me. "Our conversations were in confidence," he said. "I cannot help you."

I also got to my feet. "Cannot, or will not?" I asked curtly.

"As you please," he said, and smiled.

Flushed with anger, I made for the door. Just before I passed into the open air, he stopped me by speaking my name.

"I will tell you this much," he said when I had turned. "Your lady did not come to me with grief for her deceased husband or mother. To the best of my recollection, she did not even mention such losses. Her problem is of a more serious nature. Her concern is with the living, not the dead."

This said, Denisov returned to his chair, picked up his pen and began to write, his head lowered over his papers. With a farewell, I left him.

On the way to my coach, I was forced to walk among

the unfortunates. How twisted and ugly and vile are their appearances! There is something odd about them—as there is about Denisov himself. I don't know why, but I was compelled to reach into my pockets and disperse a handful of coins. While they groveled for my offering, I climbed into my carriage and instructed the driver to return me to the inn.

Before we had pulled away, however, I saw Denisov step onto the stoop of his shack. He stood with arms outstretched as if to envelop his followers. The sun broke through the clouds and suddenly bathed the knoll in a bright, glaring light which seemed to feed life into his colorless robe.

Heaven, or Hell?

I felt a shiver run the length of my spine and settle about my heart.

"Hurry!" I yelled at the coachman. "Drive on!"

Emile was waiting for me when I returned to the inn.

He had, as instructed, approached Lady Hargrave's maid.

"She considers herself most fortunate," he told me, "to have secured a position with a lady such as her mistress. She is from a poor family and expected no more of life than to toil in the public laundries."

"My interest does not lie with the maid," I informed him curtly.

Emile ignored my comment. "Her name is Sarah," he continued. "She is talkative, but I feel her knowledge of her mistress is limited. She was employed only two days before the journey."

"Two days?" How strange, I thought, for a lady such as Lady Hargrave, who must have had numerous maids at her beck and call, to have employed someone unknown to serve her while away from her home. "To what," I asked Emile, "does she attribute her stroke of good fortune? How did she come to be employed by Lady Hargrave?"

Emile looked at me shrewdly. He saw that my interest was sparked. Cocking his handsome head to one side, he smiled at me and said nothing.

"Well?" I demanded.

"Sarah," he said, "is not what one would call comely. I was forced to appeal to her feminine side. In short, to make it clear that I wanted her. Desperately."

I stared at him dumbly.

"Even for a Frenchman to follow through with such a commitment is not easy without incentive," he said. "And if we are to learn all you wish to know about this lady, I will surely be forced to follow through with her maid."

"In short," I said, "you want higher pay before you embark on a romantic escapade."

"Sarah is bony, unattractive," he told me, and worked his mouth into a grimace. "I might not do my best when it profits me so little."

If money affected his virility, I had no course but to agree to his demands. I had learned nothing from Denisov, and the maid's information might prove invaluable.

After an agreement had been made, Emile settled himself in a chair like a guest and helped himself to a glass of wine. "According to Sarah," he said after wetting his lips, "her mistress is very secretive."

"I am already aware of that fact," I stated flatly.

"She is not even certain if her mistress is a good Christian." He laughed. "That's important to Sarah, you see? She told me her mistress does not say morning prayers, and her night prayers are never performed until midnight or later." He took another sip of wine and continued, "But next to godliness is cleanliness, again according to Sarah. Lady Hargrave never wears the same garment more than once. It is rendering her maid's hands sore with a rash."

"I am not paying you to hear a maid's lament," I said curtly.

Emile smiled. "Indeed not," he said. "Lady Hargrave, it seems, puzzles her maid by spending hours with various books and charts."

"What kind of books? What kind of charts?" I was searching for a common interest which I could use to approach my friend's elusive sister.

Emile's brow furrowed into a frown. "Sarah thinks the books are concerned with recipes and stars." He shrugged. "The poor creature can't read or write."

I sank into a chair, despondent. Each avenue seemed a dead end. It seemed the only one who could tell me anything about Lady Hargrave was Lady Hargrave herself.

Emile broke into my thoughts. "I got the merest glance at one of the books."

My head shot up with hope. "And?" I demanded.

"I think," Emile said, "that it was indeed involved with

the stars. I have seen such drawings as the one in the book in the home of an . . . an . . ."

"Astrologer?" I pressed.

Emile nodded. "My mother was addicted to astrologers and gypsies and mystics."

I sat staring thoughtfully at the floor. Astrology, I kept repeating to myself. And the messiah, the mystic, Denisov. Lady Hargrave was obviously interested deeply in the occult.

Perhaps through that interest lay my introduction.

Emile continued to babble, but I scarcely listened.

By afternoon I had decided on a means of attracting Lady Hargrave's interest in me. Since she seems so taken by things pertaining to the occult, I sent Emile to a nearby shop for a packet of tarot cards. I missed lunch in order to study the accompanying brochure, and before the guests had left the dining room, I stationed myself at an obvious vantage point in the lobby with the cards spread out on the table before me. Anyone leaving the dining room for any other part of the inn would have to pass me.

Lady Hargrave was, as I had expected, one of the first to pass through the lobby. She noted my presence and immediately began to move away. Before she reached the stairway, however, she paused, turned and retraced her steps. She stopped beside my chair, and although I could see the hem of her gown, I pretended to be completely occupied and unaware of her presence.

Turning a card thoughtfully, I heaved a sigh and leaned back in my chair. When it was time to recognize her, I had no difficulty in registering surprise. Although she still wore the dress of mourning, she had eliminated her customary veil. Its absence increased her appearance of fragility; it also revealed her beauty more openly. Something strange happened within my chest. My heartbeat quickened, and I became aware of the pulse at my temples. I felt as if all strength had been drawn from me. I could only sit and stare at her like an idiot—or should I say a loving pet?

She did not appear to notice my rudeness. Her gaze was fixed on the table of cards.

"Are you capable of reading the future, Monsieur Laurent?" she asked softly.

I managed to rise. "An inheritance from my late mother," I told her, and laughed modestly. "One that does me little good, but intrigues me nevertheless."

"Was your mother . . . clairvoyant?"

It was the first time her voice had reflected anything except impatience with me. I knew this was my opportunity to compel her interest, to perhaps keep me in her favor until my mission could be accomplished, but I felt suddenly weak and incapable of thinking clearly. I was aware of the fragrance she wore: a musky odor that both attracted and repelled me. Her gown, in the style of the Empire, was cut low at the bodice, its blackness framing the white of her flesh. I shifted my position in an effort to overcome her hold on me and stared down at the tarot cards. If only, I told myself, she did not stand quite so near.

"My mother," I finally managed, "frightened family and friends with her strange talent."

Lady Hargrave looked at me severely. "Your tone is one of criticism," she said. "Or of jest."

"No. Neither," I said hurriedly. "I assure you I take the art of card reading quite seriously."

This seemed to appease her. She sighed and, leaning over the table, examined the cards more openly. "And you are capable of reading your own?" she said. "Isn't that supposed to be extraordinary? I am told that even the most gifted cannot read for themselves."

"I try," I told her.

"Fascinating," she said. "Have you truly inherited your mother's ability, or are you merely assuming it?"

Her frankness startled me. "I have," I lied.

"And could you do my reading?" she asked.

"I could."

Taking her hand, I assisted her into the chair across from my own. She laid her handkerchief on the edge of the table and, leaning back, folded her hands in her lap. I noted the manner in which she laced her fingers together and realized she was as nervous as she was fascinated.

"Please do not consider me a gullible fool," she told me suddenly. "If I find you to be a charlatan, I am honest enough to tell you."

I pretended indignation, but said nothing.

Passing her the cards, I instructed her to shuffle and cut them three times, using her left hand. Then, when she passed them back to me, I held them in both hands and closed my eyes for a brief moment of reflection. When I placed the cards in the pattern remembered from the brochure, I did so with dramatic slowness, watching her through lowered eyelashes.

"The knave," she said when I turned the first card. "Doesn't that signify a dishonest person in my vibration?" Her eyes grew serious, her voice dwindling to a mere whisper.

"We mustn't be hasty," I warned. I caught sight of her maid, Sarah, watching us from the door of the servants' lounge; she did not look happy seeing her mistress involved with such French deviltry.

"I apologize for my interruption," Lady Hargrave said. "Please continue, Monsieur Laurent."

Nothing more was said until nine cards had been turned up on the table in the shape of a cross. While I pretended to study their message, I was actually wondering where to begin and exactly how much of my knowledge of her life I should reveal.

"Your house," I finally began, "has recently been shadowed by death."

She smiled. "I told you that, Monsieur."

"I know," I assured her, "but it is also in your cards. I can only tell you what I see."

"Very well. Forgive a second interruption."

I feared the quick, fluttering movements at the corners of her mouth would turn themselves into a laugh. If she had laughed at me, I knew I would crumble. My composure was held together only by sheer determination.

"The death has strongly affected three persons," I continued. "An older gentleman who conceals the depth of his grief beneath a sham of bravery. A younger man, perhaps a brother, who has hurled himself into a social whirl to forget. And you, Lady Hargrave, the mostly deeply affected of the three." I drew my brows together as if puzzling over the cards. "It seems your loss was double. Ah, yes. You told me as much in our first conversation. You lost your husband and mother within a narrow span of time. That, then, is the significance of double grief."

I felt somewhat pleased with myself. Every woman likes to think of her father as brave, likes to consider his possible indifference a sham; and Charles, her brother, would most assuredly be the center of the social season in London regardless of what tragedy had befallen his family.

When I glanced up to meet Lady Hargrave's stare, she was looking at me suspiciously. Obviously, I had not pleased her as much as myself.

"A very good deduction," she said quietly. "Or one that was taken directly from the London press."

I acted as if wounded by her suggestion. "If you have no faith in me," I said, "perhaps I should not continue."

"Perhaps not, Monsieur." The old bitterness had returned to her voice. I was again no more than a bothersome fellow guest whom she had the misfortune of having to tolerate. She reached for her handkerchief and pulled it into her lap. I knew she was using it as she had used her book that morning in the garden. She was about to end our second conversation.

"An interesting thing here," I said hurriedly, pointing at the lowest card in the spread. "There is an underlying friction between all members of your house." When she did not react, I pointed quickly to the card just above the last. "And here . . . something else . . . another man in your life. The cards are vague on timing. I cannot say if you are going to meet him soon or have already met him, but he is tall, handsome, and . . . ah, yes, he is a man of power and influence."

Her eyes slightly widened with the mention of a man. Her hand abandoned her handkerchief to her lap and came to rest on the edge of the table. There was a sudden flush to her cheeks, and her bosom, lifted firmly by the style of her gown, rose and fell quickly as if she were forced to struggle against her corsets for air.

"Perhaps you yourself can supply the timing," I suggested. "Have you met such a man?"

She seemed to collect herself, and smiled. "It is you who are telling the fortune, Monsieur," she said softly.

"Very true," I conceded. "I am the fortune-teller." I sighed and leaned back in my chair. "But I fear my talent loses its adequacy for the lack of privacy. It is difficult to concentrate with so much activity about us."

She glanced about the lobby as if aware of the other guests for the first time. She gave a start when she realized an elderly couple sitting to our right had been openly listening.

"Perhaps," I suggested, "we could continue in more suitable surroundings."

She looked at me doubtfully.

"At your convenience, of course," I added.

Rising, she stood looking down at the cards as if trying to reach a decision. Seeing her like that, torn between curiosity and decorum, I realized that behind her English reserve and coolness she was having difficulty coping with our French laxity. Was she, after all, so different from most women? The mention of a man in her life had sparked her interest—but was it not the oldest prediction to be given to a young, attractive woman? As I stared at her, I remembered Denisov's telling me that her visits to him had been concerned with the living, not with the losses of her husband and mother. I somehow believed him. In fact, I was seized suddenly by the doubt that she had shed a single tear in grief over either of these persons. I had thought her mysterious, different in some unknown manner, but was she? Was she instead just a beautiful woman looking impatiently forward to her next romantic adventure? The man I had mentioned in the cards was, of course, meant to be myself. I had wanted her response, had wanted to judge possibilities.

"At your convenience," I repeated.

Her face clouded. "I do not really believe in such foolishness," she said suddenly. "My interest was only a temporary diversion from this dreadful place."

I was stunned by her obvious lie. "You criticized me because you thought I made a jest of my talent," I reminded her. "Then you call it foolishness and a mere diversion." My tone was sharp, but I meant it to be so.

Her eyes met mine, the defiance that sparked there quickly dying.

"So be it," I said with a sigh. "There is much to be revealed, but if you do not believe . . ."

"The future has a way of revealing itself, Monsieur Laurent. It is another of those things that . . ."

"That are there waiting for us, and there is nothing to be done about it," I finished.

"Exactly!"

"Not quite true," I ventured. "Knowledge in itself can begin a chain reaction that may alter our kismets."

"You really believe that, don't you, Monsieur Laurent?"

"I do, most certainly."

She lowered her head. "So do I," she said, so quietly that I almost failed to hear her. "But for quite different reasons from yours." Without another word, a farewell or a nod, she turned and moved across the lobby and up the staircase. Sarah, coming from the lounge, ran after her.

I sank back into my chair and collected the cards. My success or failure would not be known immediately—not tonight, at least. When she had had time to think about her diversion, I would either be totally rejected or be called to her rooms for a second consultation. I expected the latter.

And once alone with her in her rooms?

Would I kill her then? No, too soon! Too careless!

I must think clearly, but I was still too confused. The fragrance of her lingered beside me. The power of her smile, remembered, still caused my pulse to quicken.

No sooner had I returned to my rooms than Emile's familiar knock sounded on the door.

He was smiling broadly, a mysterious glint in his eyes. Entering my rooms, he made straight for the cognac decanter and helped himself to a brimming glass. When he had drained half the contents, he turned to me and laughed gaily.

"My friend," he said, "I believe your lady has finally taken notice of you."

My heart quickened, but I said nothing.

"Are you not even excited?" he asked incredulously. "Look! She is now sending you notes!" He removed an envelope from his breast pocket and held it up teasingly for me to see. "A declaration of love, I suspect," he said. He passed the envelope under his nostrils and closed his eyes in mock ecstasy. "Ah, how sweet the fragrance of love."

I took the envelope from him. As soon as I noticed the Hargrave seal on the flap, my hand began to tremble. I was forced to sit down at my desk before opening it.

It read:

> *M. Laurent,*
> *I find the fascination of your attempted card reading lingers with me. At your suggestion of privacy affording you a more accurate glimpse into my future, I would appreciate receiving you in my rooms this evening at nine o'clock.*
> *Lady Nina Hargrave*

Emile, who had been standing quietly behind me, laughed again and moved forward as if to be allowed to read the letter. I quickly folded it and returned it to its envelope.

His expression told me my action had wounded him. "Well?" he asked impatiently. "Has the lady decided she cannot live without you, Monsieur?"

"You are too romantic," I told him.

"I am merely French," he answered. "The same as you, my friend. What would life be without romance?"

"What indeed?" I shoved the envelope into my pocket and absently patted the material of my jacket above it.

When Emile saw that I was not about to share the contents with him, he became extremely moody. The spark went from his eyes, and the smile died on his lips. I suppose he felt that since he had been my conspirator, he deserved to share in the victory of my success.

"I would like to be alone," I told him.

He pulled himself up stiffly, assuming the role of valet. He stared at me for a moment, speaking only with his eyes, and then, turning, moved quickly toward the door. He paused with his hand on the knob. Glancing back at me, he said, "You are, I think, less French than I."

"I seriously doubt that," I answered. "I am not as young, but just as much French."

"When you arrived, I did not consider you as a lady's man," he said. "I thought you were . . . well, not the type to be chasing after skirts."

"I see," I said coolly. I felt as if there were a stamp somewhere on my forehead or cheek that must have declared me less of a man.

"But your obsession with the Englishwoman disproves that, does it not?"

I smiled at him tolerantly. "Do you expect me to defend myself? Or is it explanations you are seeking?" His long leave-taking was beginning to irritate me.

"My apologies, Monsieur Laurent," he mumbled with formality, and nodded his head in the manner of a proper valet. "I was under the delusion we had become something of friends. I will not make the mistake again. You are the master and I your well-paid lackey. But before I leave you . . ." His voice was low and cold, and his attitude made him appear even younger than his eighteen or nineteen years. He hesitated—waiting, I suppose, for me to come to my senses and apologize for my rudeness.

I lowered my gaze, feeling more like a father figure than I had at any other time in my life. I had not meant to offend him, but with thoughts of Lady Hargrave occupying the better part of my mind, I did not feel free to consider my relationship with the inn valet. I wanted to be alone to consider the possibilities of tonight's meeting with Lady Hargrave, to prepare a second reading of the tarot.

I managed a convincing smile, and told myself he would have to content himself with that for the present. "Give me your information, Emile," I said quietly. "We will talk later, when I am in a better frame of mind."

This seemed to appease him. The muscles of his face relaxed, and when he opened the door his movements were less stiff. "It may be of no importance," he said, "but . . ."

"But what?" I pressed when he hesitated.

"I managed a glimpse of another of Lady Hargrave's books while I was visiting Sarah," he told me.

"More astrology?"

"No," he said, puzzled. "The book had no title."

"Perhaps it had worn off," I suggested.

He shook his head. "Neither did it have a title page. It was not printed in English, or French, or any language of which I have any understanding."

I shrugged away his expectation of an explanation. "It

only proves we are dealing with a very intelligent lady," I told him.

But after he had gone, his information continued to nag me.

Was it possible for a very intelligent woman, a woman familiar with several languages, to truly be taken in by a simple foretelling of the future such as I had given her earlier?

Lady Hargrave was a creature of contradictions.

I have the balance of the afternoon before me. I have studied the brochure that accompanied the tarot cards; I have made notes. I have committed suitable words to memory.

I will not go down to dinner. I could not bear to sit at the table next to Lady Hargrave's, pretending to enjoy my meal while my stomach cramped and balked at each bite. My palms perspire more than they did when I killed my first soldier on the field of battle; more than when I was forced to assist the regimental surgeon to amputate a man's arm; more even than when I killed my wife's lover.

Jacqueline! If it had not been for you, I doubt that I would find myself here now. And where are you? What gentleman's bed are you favoring with your fickle warmth?

I will make use of this creeping time to write of my first trip to London, my mission of revenge. I will not record the difficulties in crossing the Channel, of bribing boatmen, or finding English clothing in the back rooms of Parisian tailor shops. These things seem hazy even now. It is almost as if they were a part of another man's life, not my own.

I remember being put ashore in the dead of night miles from my destination. I walked through the countryside in the darkness, finally securing a lift near dawn in the back of a delivery wagon. In London itself, I risked asking directions from an old lady in a chemist shop. Fortunately, she did not question my accent, possibly because of faulty hearing or a complete lack of interest in the war. She directed me to the address on the envelope I showed her.

The street was in a better neighborhood. The houses were enormous, rich, and the comings and goings of servants and tradesmen allowed me to loiter without attracting suspicion. The house of Jacqueline's gentleman was one of the largest on the block. I paced about outside the fence hoping to catch sight of him. The day passed slowly.

When I felt my passion dwindling, I would brush my hand over the breast pocket of my coat and feel the crinkle of the letter inside: the letter to my wife that I had intercepted. It was written in a sprawling masculine style, carefully phrased sentences that spoke of all-consuming love, of his withering away from want of her. He dreamed, he wrote, of her nightly, of the warm touch of her lips, the willing response of her body. He promised that the war would soon be ended. Then he would cross the Channel and carry her back to England, to God's country.

Each time I thought of the letter, my passion for revenge would rekindle itself.

Finally, just before sundown, I walked up to the door of his house and rang the bell. My hand was in my pocket, the metal of the pistol cold against my damp palm.

53

The bell was answered by a young serving girl with cow eyes and drab, colorless hair. She reeked of cheap cologne water and had the irritating habit of biting her lower lip between words. When I inquired for her master, she informed me he had left the city for a weekend of country air and hunting. She refused flatly to give me his country address and told me that if I left my card she would see that he received it immediately upon his return. I declined, and she closed the door in my face.

I felt I could not return to Paris. The crossing had been expensive as well as dangerous. Once at home, I feared I would become docile again. I did not want that to happen. My revenge somehow seemed to be related to my own freedom. If I did not succeed in killing my wife's English lover, I would remain her prisoner until the day I died.

Such were the thoughts racing through my mind as I left the Englishman's house and walked without direction. When I came to my senses, I was forced to smile at myself. Like a horse returning to its stable, or a dog to its hearth, I had found my way to the docks. There would be few questions asked of me there. Curiosity was not healthy among thieves and cutthroats and deserters.

I located an inn, took a room and then went into a pub with the intention of quick and obliterating intoxication. Leaving on my cape and hat, I stationed myself at a corner table, ordered brandy and sat drinking quietly with my thoughts. I had had two, perhaps three glasses of the foul-tasting liquid the English refer to as cognac when a gentleman approached my table, sat without being asked and ordered a bottle and two glasses.

When the bottle and glasses were brought and it was obvious the second glass was meant for me, I pushed it aside and said that I preferred to remain alone.

"But no one should drink alone," he told me. His voice was pleasant, cultured, but something about his eyes alarmed me.

With my head lowered, I stared at him from under the brim of my hat. He was perhaps ten years my senior, distinguished and obviously a man of means. His hair and moustache were black, streaked with gray, his eyes blue and expressive. There was a mole on his left cheek and a purplish birthmark at the corner of his right eye. He had the habit of tilting his head slightly to one side as he spoke.

He introduced himself as Charles Arledge.

I remained silent.

"If you should agree to drink with me, then neither of us will be forced to drink alone," he continued.

I decided that there was something about him—something about his fine manners—that I found becoming. Although he was forward, for what reason it was not apparent, his expression hinted at an expected rejection. He was, I reasoned, as much the outcast as I had become in the past years since my marriage. If he was not, then why would such a refined gentleman be forced to seek friends among the lowliest of his countrymen?

On impulse, I reached for my glass and pulled it back to me. "To not drinking alone," I said.

Laughing, he filled our glasses, and we drank.

Despite his breeding and status, I felt a bond with this stranger. Perhaps this bond, this common denominator which had drawn him to my table, was loneliness. He talked openly, excitedly, like a man starved for companionship, speaking of the war, Lord Nelson's latest victory, of the changing fashion, the poetry of Lord Byron and the paintings of Gainsborough, whom he claimed to admire more than the modernists. He did not seem to notice that my comments were limited to nods and grunts and senseless laughs. His need for male companionship, regardless of the lack of exchange between us, seemed to be satisfied.

By the time we had poured the last of the liquor into our glasses, my head was reeling and my tongue loosened. I lost concern for my accent, for the danger that threatened me should it be discovered that I was a Frenchman. I began to relate comic tales, translating them as well as my thickened tongue would allow. I boasted of past escapades, some real and others borrowed from comrades, and even told him the story of past love affairs. This, of course, reduced me to drunken tears, and my new friend, taking my glass away, suggested we call it a night.

I refused.

The more liquor I had consumed, the more attractive the serving girl had become to me. My eyes followed her from table to table as she attended the thinning crowd of drinkers. She was young, perhaps my own age, with blond hair and dark eyes. Her face, although not unattractive, did not match the splendor of her body: the thin waist, heavy hips and ample breasts that moved freely inside a revealing blouse. She was aware of my interest and kept turning to smile at me.

"Her name is Stella," Charles Arledge suddenly said at my elbow. "Do you want her?" There was a tinge of distaste in the tone of his voice. "She can be had for a price."

Irritated, I asked, "Are you her pimp?"

He laughed at my insult. "No, my friend. I am no woman's pimp." He laughed again and lifted his glass to his lips, drained it and set it in the middle of the table. "I had thought you understood me," he said. He lifted his hands, shrugged and sighed. "Ah, well, another night, perhaps."

As he pushed back his chair to rise, I said, "I did not intend to offend you. It's the drink talking, not the man that I am."

He hesitated and gave me a lingering look. After a moment, he relaxed in his chair once again. "If you wish," he said, "I can arrange a little party." He nodded toward the barmaid.

Before I could answer, could protest, he went on, "With your handsomeness and youth, I doubt that Stella would decline such an offer. If you look about this pub, you'll see her usual clients."

I felt suddenly cornered. My sexual doubts, those I blamed on Jacqueline, returned. I stared at the barmaid, considering her in a strictly sexual manner. The thought of her in bed with me excited me, but I had been excited numerous times with my wife and had then been incapable all the same when the moment of test had arrived.

Charles Arledge leaned across the table and laid his hand gently on my arm. "I'll tell her you are a lonely Frenchman who has been overwhelmed by her beauty," he whispered into my ear.

My panic must have shown on my face.

"Have no fear of me, my friend," he said calmly. "I am not going to call a policeman or announce your presence to the crowd. I bring up your nationality only to prove to you that I am to be trusted."

I felt somewhat sobered and cursed myself for having indulged my desire to become intoxicated. "I am here on a personal matter," I told him. I cursed Jacqueline; I cursed her English lover. I could visualize myself rotting in an English prison or standing before a firing squad.

Charles Arledge stared at me without speaking.

"I do trust you," I finally told him. What choice did I have? My fate now rested with this stranger who had befriended me.

He asked me if I was staying at the inn and excused himself when I admitted I was. I watched as he made his way across the bar and approached the busy Stella. He took her arm with familiarity and whispered into her ear. She glanced my way, smiled and spoke to Charles Arledge before scurrying away to the bar with a tray of glasses.

"She'll meet us in your room," I was told when he returned to our table. "We'll leave now—ahead of her. The tavern closes in another half-hour."

I drained my glass and got shakily to my feet.

Outside, the cold night air did much to revive me. I considered darting in among the buildings and attempting to lose the man at my side, but the docks were a maze with which I was unfamiliar. I stood a chance of trapping myself in some dead-end street or alley, or stepping off into the blackness of the water. If Charles Arledge was a man to be trusted, my attempt to escape might anger him enough to yell, "Spy!" to the derelicts still roaming about the docks. Any of them would risk his life to capture me and earn the reward paid for apprehending such criminals, a reward of a pardon for their own crimes.

Unfortunately, I had left my pistol in my room, not wanting to risk losing it in my drunkenness. The man walking beside me was larger, stronger than I, and, I now realized, he had consumed far less of the bottle than I. I had little chance of physically overpowering him.

"You are still apprehensive," he said suddenly. "Still afraid of me because I know you are a Frenchman. You are naive, my friend. You should become a better judge of human nature."

I readily agreed.

As we walked, he continued on the topic: "Understanding the nature of our fellow men—and women—is far more important than any other aspect of one's education. I should predict they will one day be teaching just that subject in the better institutions."

Again I readily agreed, thinking what complications and heartaches I would have been spared if I had possessed such an understanding—if only of myself.

We continued toward the inn, our heels clicking on the cobblestones, my apprehensions beginning to subside.

In my room, a shabby square with a bed, one chair and a bureau, Charles Arledge produced a second bottle and a glass from the folds of his greatcoat. Although I lifted the glass to my lips, I only moistened them with the bitter liquor and made a show of swallowing. I passed the glass back to him, removed my cape and sank to the edge of the bed, feeling some comfort in knowing my pistol was under the corner of the mattress should the next moment produce the authorities outside my door.

Charles took the only chair, stretching out his legs and

resting his feet on the metal frame of the bed. He drank directly from the bottle. This action rid me of my final apprehension. If he had instructed the barmaid to summon the police to my inn, he would not have wanted to be found drunk when they arrived. He began to talk once again as openly as he had talked when he had first joined my table at the tavern. Soon we were laughing and retelling stories we had already shared. I accepted a drink and welcomed the warming sensation as it reached my stomach.

We drank until the bottle was almost empty, and I succeeded in my original intent of becoming completely intoxicated. Jacqueline, her lover, everything freed itself from my mind.

"We are true friends?" I demanded of my visitor.

"True friends," he assured me.

The sounds of the morning carts on the cobblestones gave me a momentary sense of time.

"And Stella? Where is she, true friend?"

Before he could answer, I fell back on the bed unconscious.

When I awakened, my first awareness was of the effect of the alcohol. My head was throbbing, my vision cloudy. The draperies had not been completely closed, and the dim light filtering into my shabby room seemed unmercifully intense. I lay without moving, trying to gain my perspective. Slowly, thoughts of Jacqueline and my mission came back to me. Her Englishman was due to return from the country this evening. I remembered the pistol, and then Charles Arledge. My mind began to reel. I opened my eyes against the glare of the light. Our empty cognac bottle lay against the baseboard of the dingy wall, the not-quite-empty glass sitting beside it. There were boots, two pairs, placed neatly beside one another beneath the chair.

I was jolted into awareness. Turning my head painfully, I saw that I did not occupy the bed alone. Charles Arledge slept beside me, the yellowed sheets pulled up about his chin. I tried to remember if Stella had arrived after all, arrived and departed, and if I had participated in an unlikely ménage à trois, but I could remember little beyond returning to my room. I continued to stare at Charles Arledge as if expecting him to awaken suddenly and confirm all that had happened, but he slept deeply.

Quickly and quietly, I dressed and left my room.

That night when Jacqueline's lover returned from the country, he did not see the inside of his grand home. I waited for him in the shadows of his yard, waited crouched within the hedges until he had climbed down from his carriage and dismissed the coachman. Then, stepping forward and calling my wife's name, I drew the pistol from beneath my cape.

Startled, he made a whining sound in the base of his throat. My pistol and the reason for wanting him dead filled him with panic. Spinning about, he made an attempt to reach the street. I fired the pistol. He threw his hands into the air, stumbled and with a piercing cry, fell face down into the gutter.

The street, quiet until that moment, suddenly came to life with activity. Windows and doors were thrown open. Voices were raised in questioning cries and were answered by the shrill whistle of a policeman. I could hear footsteps running toward the scene, but I made no effort to flee. Like one drained of purpose, I merely stood waiting to be apprehended.

Then Charles Arledge was miraculously at my side. I didn't know where he had come from—perhaps a hiding place nearby where he had witnessed the entire scene. He took the pistol from my hand and shoved it into his own waistband, covering it with his coat.

"Leave everything to me," he said quietly. "Everything!"

I stared at him in bewilderment.

A smile broke on his face. "André, my true friend," he said, "your tongue is easily loosened by drink. You have told me everything about this man. He is my cousin." Slapping me on the shoulder in a congratulatory manner, he added strongly, "The bastard needed killing."

He left me alone, practically on his cousin's stoop, and moved forward to meet the policeman. Together they pulled his cousin's body from the gutter. Charles bent and examined it, announcing to the policeman that the victim was indeed dead.

From where I stood, still stunned by my act, I could hear Charles explaining the incident to the officer. He told him we had chanced by as his cousin had been arriving by carriage. We had started up the walkway to greet him when a ruffian had suddenly stepped from the bushes. Surprised by us, the scoundrel had becomed panicked, had fired the fatal shot and had then darted away between the houses.

"My friend," he said, nodding toward me, "is in a state of shock. I must get him home before we have a second death on our hands."

The policeman obviously knew Charles Arledge well. He made no effort to stop us when he came back for me, took my arm and helped me to his waiting carriage. As we drove away through the gathering crowd, he sighed with satisfaction and slapped me laughingly on the leg.

"Your wife is yours again, my friend," he announced. "And many other wives have been left without a lover." He threw back his head and laughed loudly. "I could not tell you how many will be grieving tomorrow when they get the news. Or how many husbands will be thanking you."

I slumped in the corner of the carriage, closed my eyes and attempted to still my trembling.

Charles Arledge hid me in the basement of his father's house until arrangements were made to smuggle me back into my own country. He visited me regularly in that damp basement room, and I soon became accustomed to his strange, often macabre sense of humor, his lapses into moody silence when we would merely sit together and drink without conversation.

My return to Paris proved the entire incident over Jacqueline to have been futile. Not one to be left alone to brood for any period of time, she had met another gentleman. In the farewell note she left me, she claimed a deep and binding love for her new paramour and told me living without him would be an impossibility. He was an officer, ironically one with whom I had had dealings when I had made arrangements for his regiment, and he had taken her with him to his post in Spain, where Napoleon's brother Joseph was fighting for permanence of his crown.

Not only had Jacqueline taken her personal items; she

had also had the foresight to dispose of our furnishings as well. The life of a camp follower, even the camp follower of an officer, must have caused her to collect every franc possible. While I gathered my meager belongings to seek other lodging, I chanced across her love letters from her murdered Englishman. She had left them in a drawer of a sagging bureau with the now dried-up rose petals that had kept her garments fresh.

I adjusted rapidly to my desertion. Once I knew Jacqueline was removed from my life, I was even glad to be rid of her and made party jokes about her having become a camp follower. Fortunately, the loss of one's wife had become chic with the social crowd, despite a sudden surge of directives from the Emperor himself to comport ourselves with greater dignity. I resumed my charade as a gentleman of distinction and was in demand as a guest by Parisian hostesses.

As soon as the war with England ended, I took to crossing the Channel as often as possible to seek out Charles Arledge's companionship. We spoke of his murdered cousin on only one occasion. He told me I should not regret having killed him; I had surely made the world a better place.

As for the gun, he told me he had thrown it into the Thames.

During one of those long evenings while hidden in the Arledge cellar, after Charles and I had drunk ourselves into our usual stupor, I apparently wrote and signed, in jest, a confession of my crime.

He must have goaded me into such foolishness.

As much time as I have spent with Charles Arledge, I

have not yet truly come to understand the workings of his mind. He would say that I have no more of an understanding of human nature than on the night we met. He would possibly be accurate in thinking this. It is regrettable. I would like to understand what perverse sense made him demand his sister be degraded before dying.

But he has not given me the right to question.

I am as much the servant as Emile.

If my performance is worthy, I shall be rewarded.

If it is not . . . !

Lady Hargrave's rooms are larger, more elegant than my own. They have been lavishly decorated in the furnishings of Louis XVI, a period that has not yet regained full favor in France. The color scheme consists of roses and pinks, and suits, I think, its present mistress.

A somber Sarah opened the door for me and saw me into the drawing room. Sarah greatly disturbs me. I watched her closely as she withdrew, but saw nothing in her movements or attitude to warrant suspicion.

Alone, I took the opportunity to become familiar with my victim's surroundings. The doors of the armoire were slightly opened. I could see luggage stacked neatly within. The tabletops were highly polished, a testament to Sarah's efficiency. Each held a small vase of seasonal flowers. Turning in my chair, I saw the writing desk. It showed evidence of recent use. Several sheets of stationery were tucked into a corner of the blotter. The wire receptacle beneath was filled with crumpled sheets of the same pale pink paper as that of the note I had received.

I did not think so many sheets would have been wasted to pen my simple invitation. Then to whom did Lady Hargrave find such difficulty writing? Convinced I would find needed information, I moved quickly to the closed door and pressed my ear against the carved wood. There were no sounds from beyond. Even with all the time I had spent writing in my journal, I was a few minutes early for our appointment, and Lady Hargrave, being true to a woman's nature, had not been prepared to receive me. Thinking it safe to investigate, I hurried to the waste receptacle and withdrew several of the crumpled sheets. Two were completely without writing; one had a date approximately six months in the future: May 30 and the year. Above the date was written the astrological sign *Gemini*. The fourth sheet was more revealing.

Charles, it began.
I am outraged! How dare you plant . . .

The writing broke off in mid-sentence.

I stared at the remaining sheets in the bottom of the basket, but I dared not dig deeper without risking discovery. I recrumpled the four sheets and returned them to the receptacle. I was about to return to my chair when my eye caught the corner of an envelope protruding from beneath the edge of the blotter. I lifted the blotter, careful not to upset the inkwell, and saw that the letter was addressed to Mr. Charles Arledge, London.

The style of penmanship was not as neatly executed as in my note. It was as if her fingers had been gripped by fitful nerves or—as she had stated on the discarded sheet—

by outrage. What, I wondered, had Charles done to earn her wrath? Or more accurately, what had he done that she had managed to perceive? If I could have been allowed time to open the envelope, I knew I would discover an important key to the mystery of the writer, but such an invasion was out of the question. I suddenly remembered my last episode of tampering with someone else's mail—Jacqueline's—and a shiver went through my body.

No sooner had I reseated myself than the drawing-room door opened and Lady Hargrave entered. I had never seen her attired in anything except the black of mourning, and I admit I was stunned. Her gown was the palest pink, the skirt full and flowing. Her cheeks had been lightly rouged and her lips tinted the same shade of pink as her gown. A diamond clip held her hair away from her face.

"Monsieur Laurent," she greeted me. "How punctual you are. I like that in a man."

I took her hand and pressed it gently to my lips, bowing slightly. "How could I be otherwise," I said, "when the appointment is with so charming a hostess?" I fought to still my quickened breath. Charming? She was exquisite!

"French flattery," she said, smiling. "I have not basked in it since leaving London."

"Ah, you knew a Frenchman in London," I observed. "I am envious."

Lady Hargrave removed her hand from mine. "Merely a shopkeeper," she told me. "But pleasantly flattering." She moved to the love seat and seated herself.

The flare of her skirts prevented my sitting beside her, and I quickly thought she had selected this particular gown from her wardrobe for that very reason. I sat opposite her. Taking the cards from my pocket, I placed them on the table between us.

She stared expectantly at the cards, but once I had produced them, I proceeded to ignore them. I would, I thought, use the cards as she had used her book and handkerchief, only for the reverse purpose. When she saw that I had no intention of beginning straightaway, she offered me wine, which I accepted.

After I had wet my lips and parched throat, I crossed my right leg over my left knee and appeared to make myself comfortable. I hoped she realized I had no intention of being used and then hastily dismissed.

"Have you seen the man they are calling the messiah?" I asked suddenly.

Lady Hargrave flinched slightly, then nodded.

"Of course," I went on, "there are those who call him a mystic, even a discipline of the Devil. I could not resist seeing him for myself. He is an odd fellow. I've been troubled since our visit."

Her eyebrows lifted almost imperceptibly. "Troubled in what way, Monsieur Laurent?" she asked, her question sounding as if it were asked in politeness, not curiosity.

"I cannot really explain," I told her. I sipped my wine and then stared thoughtfully into the glass.

"I consider him to be a devoted man," she said.

"Devoted . . . perhaps," I mumbled. "But devotion to religion does not make him a messiah. Even before Christ there were countless prophets who claimed to be the expected one."

"Expected." She repeated the word, more to herself than to me, and seemed to be considering it for some possible hidden meaning. She turned her attention back to me and said, "To my knowledge, Monsieur Laurent, Aleksandre Denisov has never made claim to being this messiah which . . . which you make reference to. That, I believe, is what the villagers call him. A man cannot be held responsible for what others think of him."

I had not expected to banter words with her over Denisov. I wished I had not mentioned him. Perhaps it was my curiosity over her visits that had prompted me to do so. I would apparently be left to puzzle out her reasons for seeking him out on my own; she did not appear willing to offer them.

"Then why," I asked, "doesn't he deny the title publicly?"

She set her glass aside, the wine untouched, and folded her hands in her lap, looking at me intently as she did this. "You remind me of someone of my acquaintance," she told me. "He puts great stock in public images. He thinks a man should be judged on his image, not his true self."

I assumed she spoke of her brother Charles.

She smiled and slightly tossed her head as if to dismiss an unpleasant thought. "You do not appear a religious man, Monsieur Laurent."

It was both a statement and a question.

"I am not," I confessed. "I am curious. Curious about life, about people."

"About me?"

"Indeed about you," I ventured. "Curiosity is enough of a religion for me." I made my countenance as casual as her own. Then I added, more seriously, "Pleasure! Curiosity and pleasure are my religions."

I expected to shock her, but I did not succeed. A secretive smile played about the corners of her mouth. She thinks, I thought, that I am jesting with her.

"And has your search for pleasure made your life a happy one?" she asked bluntly.

"It is easier to lose oneself in the simplicities of pleasure than in the complexities of religion," I answered.

She stared at me from under half-hooded eyes. "Is this what troubles you about Aleksandre Denisov?" she asked. "That his life is devoted to complexities while yours is the opposite?"

"Perhaps," I replied without conviction.

"Perhaps there was something else about him you found disturbing?" she suggested.

I felt that she was pressing me. I felt ill at ease, struggling within myself to find the answer she sought from me. "I sensed that there was . . . was evil about him," I finally told her.

She smiled at me, reminding me of my mother when she had been patiently tolerant of my boyhood statements. But there was something else lurking in Lady Hargrave's eyes, something beyond tolerance. "Have you ever considered that evil, like beauty, might be in the eye of the beholder, Monsieur Laurent?" She did not allow me the opportunity to reply. "Besides," she went on, "evil such as you suggest should not disturb you. You informed me you were not a religious man. This sort of evil would suggest demons and devils—perhaps the Devil himself. If you have no belief in God, belief in the Devil would be impossible. One must surely be inseparable from the other, must it not?"

I nodded almost dumbly.

By astounding me with her reasoning powers, Lady Hargrave also surprised herself. She had obviously not meant to be drawn into our topic of conversation. In a time, progressive as it might be, when it was unusual for a woman to read and write, to understand politics or discuss religion, she had unveiled herself to me as more than a beautiful, feminine creature meant to be admired by men.

She sat silently for a moment while I finished my glass of wine. Then, leaning forward as if to share an intimacy, she asked, "Are you truly curious about me, Monsieur Laurent?"

I assured her that I was.

"Then," she said with a sudden laugh, "why don't we get on with the tarot reading and satiate your curiosity?"

I could do nothing but acquiesce. I reached for the deck of seventy-eight cards and handed them to her.

"Do I shuffle three times as before?" she asked.

I nodded.

During her occupation with the cards, I took the opportunity to move my chair closer. We were sitting so near to each other that I needed only to flex my leg to touch her.

She returned the cards, and I turned them on the table in the shape of a cross. Even for one less than an amateur with the tarot, I found the arrangement of her cards mysterious. The center card was a maiden, the four surrounding cards knights. Four knight cards in a deck of seventy-eight, and all four lay staring up at me. Remembering the brochure, I turned two additional cards—a fool and the skeleton of death with its scythe raised above its head.

Lady Hargrave was also struck by the strange arrangement of her cards. She drew in her breath and her eyes widened, but she said nothing. She stared at the cards like one mesmerized. Perhaps, I thought, she has herself toyed with the tarot.

"I would make a confession," I said.

She lifted her gaze and met mine.

"My talent is not with the cards," I told her.

"But . . ."

"The cards are merely an instrument, a focal point," I explained hurriedly. "I rely on them to capture your concentration while I search for a mutual plane, our meeting sphere. If I succeed, my reading might be helpful to you. If not, then I will be reduced to scattered fragments which may prove worthless."

"What must I do to assist?" she asked.

"Merely concentrate on the cards," I instructed her. "And," I added, "it might be of assistance if we had contact. Perhaps if I could hold your hand during the reading?"

I expected her to decline such a familiarity, but she extended her hand without hesitation. I closed my fingers about it firmly and pretended to concentrate on the cards or some mythical sphere while, in fact, my mind was taken up by nothing beyond the effect of her touch. My body's chemistry seemed to be thrown into turmoil. Although it was a cold night and the room inadequately heated, the air seemed to be burning within my lungs; my forehead became damp, and specks of light darted about behind my closed eyelids. Willing myself to come to my senses, I leaned over the table of cards. I found myself studying the back of her hand; the skin was taut, remarkably pale and almost, it seemed, translucent. The silence was so complete that a conversation of two guests reached us from the courtyard below. The intrusion seemed to revive me.

"Evil!" I said.

Although my voice had been scarcely more than a whisper, its suddenness exploded in the room with the force of a shout. Lady Hargrave started and made as if to pull her hand free of mine. I did not relinquish my grasp.

"Evil!" I repeated. "You are living within the vibration of an evil force." I pretended to keep my eyes closed, but watched her through lowered lashes. "Evil! Evil! Evil!"

Her eyes widened, and once again her jaw fell slightly open. Her fingers closed with my hand, the nails biting into my flesh. It could not have been merely the summoning of her aristocratic bravado that explained the change in her expression. In a voice that did not seem to be her own, she said, "Yes! Evil! The ultimate evil!" Then she shook herself, the expression changed . . . she was herself again.

"The force is definitely masculine," I told her. "I sense a . . . a man of importance. He is to be avoided. If not, he will force you to break the rules of your English society. There will be scandal, humiliation, disaster. There will grow within you the . . ."

"Enough!" she cried. She tore her hand from mine and drew it back against her body as if it had been severely burned. There was fear and confusion in her eyes.

I was bewildered. I had expected her to laugh at my prediction. I had decided on this approach only in order to judge my own possibilities with the project. Why should she, usually cool and collected and master of conversations, suddenly give into fear at the outrageous prophecy? How far could I press her?

"Another vibration," I said hurriedly. "I also sense a rejection of you by . . . by whom, I cannot say . . . but if you are not protected by your devotions, you will face days—nay, months—of agonizing loneliness and despair. You will be . . ."

"Enough! No more, please!" She leaped to her feet, the skirt of her gown catching the leg of the table and upsetting it.

Dumbfounded, I sprang to my feet and, taking her arm, guided her back onto the love seat.

"Forgive me?" I pleaded.

She made an effort to compose herself. Although I knew she wished me to take my leave, I seated myself again, this time pushing her skirt to one side so that I might sit beside her.

Give me inspiration, I prayed. The next moment could mean my success or failure. I could imagine myself coldly expelled from her life, someone to fear and shun because of my charade as a tarot reader who had seen what fears it would have been best to leave hidden. But why?

"You were only amusing yourself with me," I said quietly, my voice heavy with mock injury. "You did not believe in my ability, and something I said proved you mistaken."

Her expression confirmed my assumption.

"If I could retract my words, I would most gladly," I told her. "Better that you continue to consider me a charlatan than for me to upset you like this."

She lifted her head and opened her mouth to speak, but

before the words could be formed there was a quick knock on the drawing-room door. It burst open, and a questioning Sarah, drawn by the noise, stood in the frame, her eyes taking in the overturned table and scattered cards.

"An accident," her mistress told her coolly. "You may straighten later."

Dismissed, Sarah withdrew and closed the door.

Lady Hargrave rose and, walking to the window, stood gazing into the darkened courtyard with half-sight. After a moment, she said, "I seem to have lost my ability to cope. In the past three months, my nerves have grown progressively more exposed." She glanced at me over her shoulder, then turned back to the window. "I tell you this because I want you to understand it is unlike me to behave as I just did."

"The blame was mine," I said.

"No, the blame rests elsewhere, Monsieur Laurent. Perhaps my condition is common in women such as myself." She turned her head so that she was visible to me in profile. "You spoke of a rejection. I have already felt the weight of it."

"From whom, my dear lady?" I inquired. "What man could possibly reject you?"

When she spoke again, her words were more guarded, obviously carefully chosen and, I felt, slightly tinted with untruth.

"I am twenty-five," she said. "I am the widow of a childless marriage. That, Monsieur Laurent, has earned me something of a rejection from my father."

"Surely you misinterpret his emotions," I suggested. "Perhaps he simply does not know how to express his grief for you over the loss of your husband. That followed by his own loss . . ."

"You do not know my family, Monsieur. My father is driven by the obsession that the Arledge line continue."

I knelt and began gathering the cards from the carpet. "I should think his hopes would lie with the male, your brother," I said. "Men with such an obsession generally attach as much importance to their name as to their bloodline."

She sighed and was silent for a moment before saying, "Perhaps I do misinterpret my father. But there is also the gossip about me in London. Absurd as it may be, it wounds me to be the victim of such vicious falsehoods. It has helped to bring me close to my wit's end." She drew the draperies with a quick movement of her hand and, turning back into the room, forced a weak smile.

I felt a sense of wanting to protect her. I also felt curiosity. Although I would have liked nothing better than to inquire of the gossip of which she spoke, it would not have been gentlemanly. I could ask for no crumbs of information that she did not willingly offer. I attempted to promise protection and understanding with my returning smile.

Seeing I had my cards, Lady Hargrave approached me and extended her hand. "Thank you for visiting me, Monsieur Laurent." Her composure had returned as quickly as it had left her. "Of course, if such a visit were suspected in London, the gossips would have had a field day with what reputation they have left me. A lady does not receive a gentleman without a proper chaperone."

Why, I asked myself was I always being dismissed with such ease?

I bowed in acquiescence. "Since we are not in London and since my intentions are honorable, I hope that we may become friends, Lady Hargrave."

"Friends." She echoed the word as if weighing it in her mind. "Yes," she said. "I have need of a friend, Monsieur. We will talk again soon."

She saw me to the drawing-room door, where Sarah, eyeing me suspiciously, materialized to escort me out.

"Goodnight, Monsieur Laurent."

I bowed low as Lady Hargrave closed herself away from me behind the drawing-room door.

Following behind Sarah, I noted her extreme scrawniness, her shapeless legs and gutter-bred carriage, and I felt a pang of sympathy for Emile. I wondered how far he had had to go with Lady Hargrave's servant in the line of duty and if the agreed sum had made the task more bearable.

Sarah opened the door and stepped aside. "Good night, sir."

I nodded and was about to pass into the hallway when I heard a door open behind me.

"Monsieur Laurent."

I turned as Lady Hargrave approached.

"One of your cards," she said, "had fallen under a corner of the love seat." She handed me the card. "Good night again."

The door was closed behind me, and I moved thoughtfully toward my own rooms. There would be much of tonight's visit that I would have to consider, much I would have to weigh and evaluate. At my door, I took out my key, opened the lock and then realized that I still carried the single card of the tarot deck in my hand.

I turned it and found myself staring at the skeleton of death.

It is very late.

I have risen from my bed and sit here with pen in hand, a coverlet wrapped about my legs. Something about Lady Hargrave nags me; something I feel I should have discerned evades me.

But what?

I cannot answer. I have gone over and over every detail of the evening. Still, I am left without insight. Perhaps it is my reaction to her that causes my sleeplessness. Why do I tremble and why does my pulse race when I am in her company? Why must I continue to think only of her when I attempt to guide my thoughts elsewhere?

Sleep—how blessed an escape it seems now that it is unattainable. I feel something of a night watchman, sitting here listening to the noises of the inn. There are others who cannot sleep this night. Several carriages have departed since before midnight. I have heard the wheels clacking over the cobblestones, fading into the quiet of the sodden night.

I wonder if Lady Hargrave sleeps untroubled—if perhaps in her dreams she has a fleeting thought of me?

I did not awaken until the sun was high. Yes—the sun! It was glorious to see it after so many dismal and depressing days. Still in my nightshirt, I threw open the draperies and stood with the warmth on my face. I felt— this morning—like a man who had wrestled with a problem and had won. This puzzled me. If I had indeed had a victory of some sort, it had been won in my dreams after sleep had finally claimed me and was out of reach of my awakened mind. Perhaps, I told myself, my exuberance was due to the fact that I had managed to fall asleep at all, that in the late hours I had finally shed the thoughts of Lady Hargrave.

I had a ravenous appetite, not having eaten the night before. I was about to ring for Emile when I spotted him in the courtyard below. He was standing about twenty yards from the gate, speaking to someone whose identity was concealed by a clump of shubbery.

Sarah, I thought, and smiled to myself. I decided that if all went well I would see that Emile was amply rewarded. Generous, too, I felt this morning.

I was about to turn away from the window when Emile suddenly bowed low, and I knew it was not the attitude he would have adopted with Lady Hargrave's serving girl. She would have giggled in his face.

Emile, turning, walked back toward the inn, his step quick and lively, and about the edge of the shrub was a glimpse of skirt—a black skirt. I caught my breath as Lady Hargrave stepped onto the path and stared after the vanishing valet.

What treachery was this? My mind jumped to several conclusions. Was Emile playing a double game? In both Lady Hargrave's and my employ? Had the Englishwoman spotted him while he visited her maid? Had she been taken by his handsomeness? Or had their meeting been a coincidence? The employees of the inn were forced to come and go through the back gate, therefore through the garden; Emile had told me that himself.

At that moment, Lady Hargrave, clutching her shawl about her shoulders, happened to glance up at my window. She smiled—no, laughed—and waved. Embarrassed at being caught in my nightshirt, I stepped back, far enough not to be seen but not too far to see myself. I saw her call out, saw Emile turn and meet her halfway along the path. They spoke for a brief moment. She pointed toward my window. Then they separated again, both returning to the inn, Emile far in advance of her.

I was still standing in the middle of the room when Emile knocked and entered. He seemed remarkably radiant this morning. Was the weather also affecting him? His hair was neatly combed, the usual curls that fell about his forehead slicked back with brilliantine. His shirt was fresh and heavily starched and his uniform new.

"Good morning, André."

This calling me by my given name was also new to him. I nodded without speaking.

"No greeting for one who brings you good news?" he asked gaily.

"And that news is?" I asked absently.

"The English lady," he said. "I chanced upon her in the garden while she was taking the air."

"I saw," I told him with a hint of anger and accusation.

His expression did not change. "She asked after your health." He fell silent for a moment, then broke the silence by laughing. "She also instructed me to ask you if you would join her for a carriage ride this afternoon." He laughed again at the manner in which I took the news.

My legs suddenly gone weak, I dropped into a chair and sat staring at him blankly. An invitation so soon . . . I had indeed made an impression. I had had a victory.

Emile, returning from the armoire with my robe, had, however, gone through a change of expression. His brow was furrowed as he handed me my robe.

"What troubles you?" I demanded. "I have made an important advance in my conquest, and you look only gloomy. Has Sarah smitten you to such a degree that you cannot sustain pleasure for me?"

"It was not your conquest of which I was thinking," he answered darkly. "The inn is buzzing with other news this morning."

"And what news might that be? Is there news from Elba? Has the throne toppled? Are we once again in the midst of revolution?" I asked these questions lightly, unable to attach seriousness to any topic for fear it would drain away the pleasure I felt with myself over Lady Hargrave's invitation.

Emile's brow did not lose its frown lines. He sank into the chair opposite mine and stared at me with troubled eyes. "Another body was found this morning," he said.

I shrugged and asked him, "Are there not bodies found every morning? The bodies of these unfortunate followers of that fanatic?"

"This was a local girl," he informed me. "She did not die of an illness. She was murdered."

How different it is in the provinces, I thought. In Paris, one was accustomed to murders and suicides. It did not startle or concern one unless he was acquainted with the victim.

"South of the village are the ruins of a church," Emile said. "There is no roof and no floor, only a few crumbling walls and a grown-over altar. The girl was found there this morning by a farmer out searching for straying stock. He says the girl was lying across the altar, her garments scattered about the ground in shreds as if they had been ripped apart by some beast."

"You dampen my mood with such talk," I said. "But why does it concern you so? Were you acquainted with the girl?"

"I knew her," he said. "She was but a child. My concern is for the manner in which she died. It is reported that the poor girl's heart had been carved from her chest."

"Gruesome," I agreed. "Some madman, most likely."

"Or madwoman," Emile suggested. "There is talk of witchcraft and devil worship. The townspeople are near hysteria, as you may well imagine. They are pointing blame at the mystic and his followers."

"Perhaps rightly so," I said.

"Yes, perhaps," Emile said uncertainly. "But my concern is for you and the English lady."

"Lady Hargrave! And me! What have we to do with the mystic?"

"It is known that both of you have visited him," he explained.

I waved away his concern. "Mere curiosity," I said. "No more. Have not most of the townspeople themselves listened to him speak? It is not merely his followers who gather on that knoll outside the village."

Emile visibly relaxed. "That is true," he agreed. "I was concerned only because some of the guests at the inn demanded their accounts when the news reached us. It appears they fear some questioning from the authorities." He got out of his chair and appeared ready to fetch my breakfast at long last. "Ah, well, my friend, you will have more privacy with your lady when these unseasonal guests depart." He winked at me and left.

But my spirits had been dampened.

Was I not planning a murder myself?

I found myself visualizing the beautiful Lady Hargrave, the clothes torn from her body, lying in a ritualistic fashion across a weed-covered altar, her heart carved from her body.

Shuddering, I put such thoughts from my mind.

When I kill her it will be with mercy. Charles will have to content himself with that!

We rode, seldom speaking, each involved with our own thoughts. Because of the recent storm and the ruts in the road, the drive did not promise to be a pleasant one. We were jostled mercilessly and were forced to hang on to the leather stirrups to keep from being thrown from our seats.

But the change in the weather had worked its magic on my companion. She seemed not to notice the ruts or the jostling. She sat gazing from the window with a look of contentment on her face. She had changed the style of her hair, forsaking the fashionable twist for an arrangement of ringlets about her left ear. There was a hint of rouge on her pale cheeks and a tint of color to her lips. Her necklace and earrings were emeralds, which possibly explained the tinge of green in her blue eyes. As I stared at her and savored her beauty, I was glad she had removed her veil as soon as we had driven away from the inn.

Soon, I reminded myself, she will be dead. Soon I will kill her. I will take her life at the command of her brother in order to save my own existence.

These thoughts came to me from nowhere and caused me to shudder and shake myself.

How perceptive she is! She turned suddenly, met my eyes and asked, "Are you ill, Monsieur?"

How I would have liked to prolong that look of concern, of sympathy. "No, no," I assured her.

"Then you were lost in your religion?"

I looked at her vacantly.

"Your religion," she repeated. "Curiosity."

Remembering, I smiled. "Indeed," I said. "Curiosity about you."

The carriage was traveling up the mountain road. Below us stretched the village, clean from a distance, and the clear, blue harbor beyond with its scattered sails. Turning her back to the scene, she asked, "What, my friend, would you like to know about me?"

"Everything," I told her.

She tossed her head with amusement. "Even I do not know everything," she said.

"Then I will settle for what you do know," I prompted. "Tell me about your childhood."

"My childhood," she mused. "I mostly remember the loneliness." Her eyes glazed over from memories called forward. "My mother married young. Three months before her eighteenth birthday, she gave birth to my brother. Rumor has it that the birth was difficult and that she almost died. She turned my father away from her bed from fear and did not allow him back for nine years. Ah, but I embarrass you with such unfeminine frankness, Monsieur Laurent."

"No, no! Not in the least." Embarrassment, no. Her frankness did, however, shock me.

She stared with half-sight through the opposite window of the coach. "I was the result of that second union," she continued. "Again my mother suffered—more with the birth of her second child than with the first, I am told. She did not, however, accept me, her daughter, with the same enthusiasm as her son. Where she doted on my brother, she ignored me. Charles represented the fulfillment of her marriage contract. I represented a night of abandonment. My upbringing was left almost exclusively to the servants. I was presented at family functions, of course, but I was always made to feel the intruder." Sighing, she lapsed into silence.

"And your brother?" I pressed. "Charles? What was your relationship with him?"

She smiled—a smile that dismissed my questioning. "My mother always said she was star-crossed. That some hostile star had passed through her chart during both of her pregnancies. Do you believe in astrology, Monsieur Laurent?"

"I do not understand the science," I confessed.

"What month and day were you born?"

"April, the thirteenth."

"An Aries," she said. "You form emotional attachments quickly. Is that so?"

I did not deny it.

"Flirtatious. A lover of adventure. With a tendency toward overindulgence." She smiled at my discomfort at being pigeonholed. "But," she added, "when an Arien decides he had met his mate, his devotion is unwavering. He abandons the life of a philanderer, forgets it as if it had never existed. He will do anything his . . ."

"And you?" I interrupted.

"Me? I am a Gemini with strong Scorpio influences," she said. "But don't expect a thumbnail analysis. I will retain a measure of mystery. I will need it in order to hold your interest." She laughed and made it impossible for me to measure her sincerity.

Hold my interest? What depths such a statement promised!

I would have pressed her further if the coach had not suddenly halted.

Lady Hargrave leaned forward and peered out of the window. "We are near Alek—the mystic's," she said with surprise.

Indeed, we were. I could see past her shoulder, see the deserted farmhouse where Denisov made his headquarters. The ramshackle building stood near the crest of the knoll, a thin stream of smoke rising languidly from the chimney. The field outside the farmhouse was dotted with the madman's followers. They packed about the porch and spilled down the knoll past the well and animal huts and into the dust of the road. Our path was blocked, and the horses, two handsome piebalds with flowing manes, were prancing nervously.

"Drive through!" I screamed at the coachman.

But Lady Hargrave, turning, laid her hand on my arm in a restraining manner. "No," she said. "Let us wait, please?"

I withdrew my instructions to the coachman and leaned back moodily in my seat. I had no desire to spend our afternoon together on a hillside listening to a fanatic preach to the sick and dying. Then I thought, But are they just the sick and dying? Are they not more? Is there not about them a disturbing aura of evil? I again thought of the child found murdered that morning and shifted my position with the discomfort of such thoughts.

Lady Hargrave, ignoring me, rested her arms on the edge of the window and stared at the farmhouse, waiting as the others waited for the appearance of the fanatical Denisov. I could not understand the alteration of her expression—the keen interest in her eyes, the firm set of her mouth. I felt something I recognized to be akin to . . . to jealousy. Denisov had stolen away my most successful moments with her. I hated him, hated him even more when I remembered his reluctance to share the reasons for her visits with him when I had questioned him. Again I asked myself, if not grief over the loss of her husband and mother, what problem had driven her to consult him?

"What are you thinking?" I asked quietly. "What thoughts have taken you away from me?"

She did not answer. Indeed, she seemed so lost to reality that I wondered if she had heard my question.

Angry, I sat sulking in my corner of the coach.

"There is talk that the authorities hold Denisov responsible for that girl's strange death last night," I finally told her in a voice that could not be ignored. "There are those who believe he is a devil."

"A devil," she echoed. She glanced at me quickly, then went back to staring from the window. "It's the age we are living in," she said softly.

"Perhaps you are right," I told her. "I blame the war. It has made men less chivalrous and people in general less respectful. They tend to look upon things with a jaundiced eye. They suspect evil where there is only harmless charlatan's play. Still, the revolution was necessary."

"Necessary," she repeated. "What has your revolution gained you, Monsieur? Equality, Fraternity and Justice! Where is justice when a man like Aleksandre Denisov might be harassed for the sake of a frightened minority? Even before the murders of these girls, the authorities wanted to run him away or imprison him. The man has done nothing. Nothing," she repeated firmly.

"But his followers have. They steal. They create disorder."

"Then arrest his followers. Or tell them to die quietly of their hunger, or where it is most convenient for the death carts to carry them away." She laughed bitterly. "Your country has not been so close to revolution since before Napoleon," she said. "You need not be French to sense the discontent. Perhaps that is why he chose to come here. Where better to plant the seeds of his . . . his religion?"

"But exactly what is his religion?" I demanded.

"More than your curiosity, you fool!" she cried.

I was rendered breathless by her sudden attack, but I could see that she just as suddenly regretted it herself. Her eyes begged my forgiveness.

A murmur rose from the crowd collecting on the hillside. I leaned forward to see Aleksandre Denisov emerge from the door of the farmhouse as he had done the day of my visit. He raised his hands, and the sleeves of his robe fell back about long, thin arms. He spoke, but we could not hear him because of our distance. Then he lowered his head, either in prayer or from the burden of emotion—I could not tell which. A man standing beside him on the porch put his arm about his shoulders, but Denisov stepped away from the embrace and moved into the crowded yard.

As he moved about the yard speaking, Lady Hargrave turned to me with a look of distraction. "I did so want to hear him," she said. She looked away before I could reply.

I stared at her profile, wondering what possible flaw in her character made her feel allied with Aleksandre Denisov and his band of unfortunate followers. She was a beautiful woman; she was wealthy. She had everything, and they nothing.

A sudden roar of protest brought me up in my seat. Soldiers were converging on the crowd from the road behind and in front of our carriage. Having surrounded the area of the farmhouse, they were now closing in, looking very much, I thought, like a regiment attacking an enemy camp.

"They have come to arrest him," I said with veiled satisfaction.

Lady Hargrave was sitting with her back straight, her expression fighting for understanding of the scene she witnessed. She reached suddenly for the door handle.

"Don't be a fool!" I pulled her hand free, knowing she would hurl herself into the confusion of the crowd and be injured.

"Why does he not save himself?" she cried.

She pulled to free herself, but I held her firmly. She spun about and was about to speak when the carriage door opened. We both stared at the soldier—a young man with a thin moustache, flushed cheeks and the smell of excitement in his flared nostrils.

"With the others!" he ordered.

Lady Hargrave, oddly willing to obey, pulled herself forward in her seat to leave the carriage, but I restrained her.

"We are not his followers," I protested to the youth. "We are the victims of circumstance. Our path was blocked and we could not pass."

The young soldier looked at me doubtfully. He had obviously not been instructed to expect persons of our appearance. The question of how he should react to us was darting about behind his eyes.

"Ask the coachman," I said hurriedly. "He can tell you we engaged him for a quiet ride in the country." Then, thinking I understood my man, I added, "A lovers' ride."

Lady Hargrave stiffened beside me, but said nothing.

The soldier turned his attention to her. She met his gaze with defiance, wanting, I suspected, to speak, to cry out a denial of my account of our presence.

The soldier's serious expression was cracked by a grin.

"A successful ride, I hope," he said. Nodding to Lady Hargrave and winking at me, he closed the carriage door.

I pounded my cane loudly on the coach floor.

The coachman screamed at his horses and cracked his whip, and the coach lunged forward.

Lady Hargrave looked stunned. "I denied him," she said incredulously. "Is it not strange? I know how Peter must have felt denying his Christ, his master."

"Better to feel like Peter than be imprisoned," I told her.

She looked at me crossly. I imagined she was considering me a coward and weakling.

The magic of the weather and our drive had been destroyed. We rode in silence, again claimed by our separate thoughts. I kept glancing at my companion hoping to find the softness returned to her face, but it retained its cold, troubled expression until we arrived back at the inn.

The coachman opened the carriage door, and I climbed down to offer Lady Hargrave my hand.

"I regret this incident," I told her. "I regret having to compromise you with a lie."

She looked at me blankly.

" 'A lovers' ride,' " I reminded her.

She stood beside me, adjusting the folds of her gown. "Earlier we were talking of my childhood," she said. "Monsieur Laurent, I remember also being a rebel. A restraining hand—or a lie meant to protect me—has never been resented once I have had time to consider it. Your actions showed that you cared about my welfare, that you are indeed my friend."

I bowed, and she walked away from me.

I would have felt better if there had been a hint of a smile in her eyes, a measure of emotion in her tone.

Sunday afternoon in the garden.

Lady Hargrave, quietly reading, turns to me abruptly. She lays her book aside and folds her hands in her lap.

"I feel nervous, uneasy. I do not know what has given it root. It is as if some ominous threat is hanging over me— some unconscious, oppressive danger. I feel clearheaded and at the same time confused. It is almost like suffering from a fever, when one feels both warm and cold at once."

I shuddered. The first thought to flash through my mind was that she had somehow come to suspect my mission, my alliance with her brother.

"Have you ever been awakened from a dream that was too horrible to permit sleep, but once awake you could not remember it?"

"I have," I said.

"That is exactly how I would describe this feeling that has me in its grip," she confided. "I can't help suspecting it is a premonition that something dreadful is about to happen to me."

I saw the worry in her face, and it alarmed me. Allowing myself the advantage of the situation, I covered her hands with my own, squeezing them gently but firmly in a promise of protection. "You need to shed the garb and thoughts of mourning," I told her with authority. "It would depress anyone to constantly wear black and to spend all but an hour or two each day in her rooms." I had not made reference to her dead husband or mother since our conversation during the carriage ride when she had confessed to being an ignored child.

She looked at me thoughtfully. "Perhaps you are right, André. It is easy to play with one's mind, to convince oneself that a mood or feeling has root in something as simple as the color of one's clothing. My mother is dead. I must bury her in both my mind and my heart."

And your husband, I thought. Have you no grief to bury with him?

I felt a movement beneath my hands and quickly pulled them away before she could shake them off. I would spare myself the rejection of physical contact.

"You are a kind man, André," she said. "You listen to my fears and have a way of driving them away with ease. I shall always be thankful for having met you." She retrieved her book from the bench and continued reading, her face averted.

What a creature of contradiction she is! I make a statement about shedding her mourning, suspecting her true feeling toward her late mother, hoping to draw out the underlying problem that plagues her, and she smothers me with agreement. Mother is dead. I must bury her in both mind and heart.

And the black attire of mourning!

Does she forget she received me that first night in a gown of pink? Does she think me the complete fool to be accepting still her sham of grief? But she does trust me—I feel it.

It is I who am both clearheaded and confused. I am the one who suffers from a strange and rising fever. It is I who have had a premonition, and it disturbs me almost beyond contemplation.

I flounder and stumble through the hours when I am away from Nina Hargrave. When I am in her company, my pulse quickens and my mind is momentarily at peace. I am consumed with the desire to possess her.

In this I must succeed soon if Charles's plan is to work.

At dinner tonight, Lady Hargrave's appearance in the dining room claimed the attention of every eye and set every tongue to wagging. Arriving late, she paused just inside the arched entrance, pretending occupation with a stubborn lace cuff but merely hesitating, I suspected, as an actor would hesitate on a corner of the stage for the full drama of his entrance to be savored before delivering the first lines of his performance. She had, as I had suggested that afternoon, shed her black mourning clothes. Her gown was a delicate blue which matched the shade of her extraordinary eyes. It was cut low in the bodice, gathered beneath her breasts and from there flowing freely to brush the nap of the carpet. When she moved, the gown teased at revealing the outline of her hips, its sheerness promising a vision of the body beneath should one be fortunate enough to catch sight of her in the proper angle and lighting. Her fingers were adorned by a single ring, lapis lazuli with a diamond mounted in its center. About her throat she wore a thin blue ribbon of the exact shade of blue of her gown.

When every eye was upon her, she proceeded to her table with the grace of a queen presenting herself to her loyal subjects. Not until the diners had gone back to their chattering did she turn and meet my gaze. There was a hint of pleasure and mischief reflected behind those pale blue crescents.

"Are you pleased, André?" she asked in a near-whisper.

"I am overwhelmed," I confessed.

"Good," she said. "You are my mentor. I dress only to please you."

"I am your slave," I told her, and stared down at the soup I had allowed to cool in waiting for her late arrival.

She laughed softly. "I have managed to shatter the image of a bereaved wife and daughter in a single appearance. Look how they steal glances and chatter like magpies."

Before I spoke again, I swallowed and was not surprised to discover my throat constricted. "I am flattered. You speak only to me, and they think me the cause of this remarkable transformation in you."

"Ah, but you are, André," she said. "You are."

When I looked at her, she had averted her eyes.

I called the waiter and ordered a glass of cognac to fortify myself. My soup was taken away untouched, as was the balance of my meal.

Lady Nina Hargrave ate with a ravenous appetite.

Emile met me in the hallway following dinner and walked with me to my rooms. He looked troubled, pale, and I inquired after his health with genuine concern.

"It is nothing," he assured me. "Perhaps a lack of rest, nothing more."

I poured him a glass of wine.

"You must take care," I warned him. "Even a young man must include sleep in his adventures. Is Sarah, then, demanding more of your nighttimes?"

He flushed. "No, not Sarah. Another lady of my recent acquaintance. Although Sarah is becoming more difficult to control." He sipped his wine. "Suspicious of me, I think," he said.

"Suspicious?"

"Curious as to my interest in her mistress," he told me. "I must guard my inquiries now. If you had not forbidden it, I would tell her a gentleman of distinction was interested in her employer. If I appealed to her sense of the romantic, she would be most cooperative. Ah, but you would know women better than I. I am but a novice in comparison." There was a hint of mockery in his tone that I did not fail to recognize.

"Such a confession would not be wise," I told him firmly. "I do not want a maid telling her mistress of my interest. It would make the entire affair reek of backstairs romance—appealing, perhaps, to a woman such as Sarah, but repugnant to a lady of Lady Hargrave's distinction."

"As you wish," Emile said abstractedly. Rising, he crossed to the window and stood gazing up at the stars through a thin mist of hovering clouds.

He is completely smitten, I thought. Whoever this new lady in his life might be, she has him in her power.

"Will you . . . will you be perfectly honest with me, André?" he suddenly asked.

"Do I seem the dishonest sort?" I retorted.

"I am young and perhaps more naive than I like to

think myself," he said, "but I am wise enough to realize that people are not always what they appear. I have been curious about you from the beginning." He turned and stood with his back to the window, and I noted the full moon past his shoulder.

"Curiosity seems to have become contagious," I said. I glanced at the clock on the mantel and saw that I had precious little time to waste with Emile. Lady Hargrave's invitation had only been alluded to in dinner conversation, but I would go to her rooms under some feeble excuse. Tonight, I told myself, might be the night of my greatest, my final success with her.

Emile came back to his chair and, to my regret, seated himself once again. He reached for his wineglass and held it without drinking, suggesting a prolonged stay. He stared at me for several moments before saying, "When I helped you unpack, I noted that your clothes were all new purchases. So too were your accessories."

I made no comment. Turning, seemingly bored, I poured myself a full glass of wine and strode to the fireplace, where I stood with my back to my young visitor.

"And when the lady who intrigues you arrived," he went on, "you appeared to be waiting for her, expecting her, although she had made no reservation and no one in the inn knew of her expected arrival."

How clever I had thought myself, and even a valet had taken note of my actions.

"Then there is the question of your insistence in wanting these particular rooms which face those of Lady Hargrave, as if aware that she would take the most expensive suite available. I daresay that from your own window you can see her movements when her draperies are not drawn."

"I am merely fond of bell towers," I said curtly. "I wanted a view of the tower and of the gardens below these windows."

"And your new wardrobe?" he pressed. "How do you explain that not one single item had had the tack stitching removed from the pockets?"

"Are you always so inquisitive, Emile? Does every man's wardrobe stimulate your curiosity?" I turned and stared down at the carpet as if drawing my questions from the pattern. "What are these questions of yours leading to? What exactly do you want to know of me?"

"It's impertinent of me, isn't it?" He drained his glass and set it aside. "I should not dare question you like this if I did not suspect that I have become involved in some sort of scheme, more than playing spy for the gods of love."

I felt my anger rise. "Your suspicions have no grounds. None whatever," I snapped. "What do you take me for? A confidence man? A fortune hunter?"

"Those things had crossed my mind," he admitted bluntly. "And more."

"Then your imagination is overactive," I assured him crossly. "Perhaps you are reading your own fantasies into my character. I, like any man, would not sneer at a lady's wealth, but I have enough of a fortune of my own to prevent me from becoming a slave for the sake of finance. My clothes are new because I have a fetish for new styles and fabrics. Why take worn apparel on a journey when one's closet is filled with the latest fashions? As for waiting for Lady Hargrave, I had never laid eyes on her until the moment she arrived at the inn." This last statement was, of course, true, and I made it with conviction. "It seems unnecessary to reveal the truths about me to one in my employ, but since you insist, I will tell you this. I am a widower. I have spent too long in mourning my late wife, and I am not getting any younger. I want the comfort of a woman—a woman such as Lady Hargrave—in my house and bed to warm the last days of my life. If you think it an intriguing possibility to consider yourself involved in some shady plot against the lady, if you think you can extract money from me—blackmail—then, my friend, you are quite sadly mistaken."

"I had no such intention," Emile assured me. The color had come to his face during my speech—my performance —and it was all too obvious that he was choking on his voiced suspicions.

I wondered if his new lady friend had helped him to devise this confrontation in the hopes of bleeding me of money—money enough to start a life elsewhere in better positions than those of servitude. As I stared at Emile, I convinced myself this was so. It was a great pity. A man as handsome as Emile could go far if he had been born with cleverness as well as physical beauty and charm. I could, however, see the future ahead of him. His life would be filled by Jacquelines. What cleverness he would possess would come with age, and then it would come on the heels of his waning handsomeness. He would end up no better than I, a pawn to his vices.

"Now you must excuse me," I told him. "I have letters to write and no wish to continue this conversation."

He rose, but seemed hesitant to take his leave. It was clear that he was upset with himself, perhaps with the woman who had put him up to this scheme of confronting me. Perhaps he was thinking I would report him to the management and he would lose his position with the inn. Whatever was on his mind, he was reluctant to voice it.

"Well?" I demanded.

"Am I still to consider myself in your employ?" he inquired quietly. "Am I still to . . . to pretend an interest in Sarah?"

I stooped and placed a log on the fire. From my squatting position, I answered without looking up at him. "If you accept the purpose for doing so," I said. "If your personal ambition does not drain away your senses and continue to plant rootless suspicions in your mind."

"I believe your motivations, André," he assured me weakly. "I should have thought things through before approaching you. It all seems so utterly stupid now that we have talked." I saw him shift his weight uncomfortably from one leg to the other. "Will you forgive me for thinking the worst of you?"

"I forgive you," I told him. Rising, I offered him my hand, which he clasped firmly.

His lips spread about white, even teeth in a childlike smile. "I have one bit of information for you," he said proudly, hoping to completely regain my favor. "We were both wondering why a lady such as Lady Hargrave would secure a servant such as Sarah."

I nodded.

"The truth is," he said, "that Sarah did not secure her position through Lady Hargrave directly. She was employed by her mistress' brother."

The shock of his information pierced me like a knife blade. Fearing Emile would note my expression and have his suspicions rekindled, I turned away, walked to the writing desk and sat down.

"Thank you, Emile. Good night."

"Good night," he answered.

The door closed behind him. I leaned forward with my elbows resting on the desktop, my face supported in my hands, and wondered how I could have been so simple as not to have suspected Charles of employing a spy to report my progress with his sister. Or, I asked myself, did Sarah have a double purpose? Had she been instructed to complete my mission should I fail? How deep did Charles's conspiracy, his evil, go?

But I have not failed. In less than an hour I have an appointment with his sister.

"So here we are, André," Lady Hargrave said, and gave me a candid smile.

I had just been shown into her drawing room and Sarah had withdrawn, possibly to spy and listen outside the door. Lady Hargrave, seated on the love seat, did not rise to greet me. She has, I thought, predetermined the flavor of this meeting. We are together without the excuse of the tarot or of an innocent carriage ride through the afternoon sun. We will not discuss fortune-telling, or Aleksandre Denisov, or the measures of one's grief; all of that is behind us.

These thoughts both rattled and comforted me.

Had she invited me here to hear my confession of emotional attachment, to hear that I could not get her out of my mind, that her face and voice followed me through my days and nights as if they had become a permanent appendage to my person?

I moved to the love seat and seated myself beside her, taking her hand and lifting it to my parched lips. "So here we are," I echoed.

Our eyes met, and she smiled. I could feel a slight return of pressure on my hand. Encouragement? A question I could not yet answer.

"You are sometimes like a small boy," she said. "At times your eyes reflect innocence and at times its opposite. One moment I believe that you are attracted to me—and the next I fear I repel you."

"Never!"

"Then you are not, as I often fear, playing a French game of emotions with me?" she asked. "You do not toy with my heart? You are not amusing yourself with me because there is no other lady in this dreary place who interests you?"

"You do me an injustice to even suggest such cruelty," I informed her. "My emotions are genuine. Beside you no lady exists."

We kissed as if we were practiced lovers.

After a moment, she pulled away from me with gentle force. She rose and reached for my hand. "Come, André, my love," she said. "A lady's drawing room is not a suitable place for this."

I followed her into her bedchamber, my mind shaken by

both excitement and a strange sense of foreboding. I have won, I told myself, but in winning I have somehow lost. I have no sense of the victor. What are the spoils? How sweet the reward of her body, but how bitter the knowledge of what fate must have in store for me. If she does not treat me as the other women in my past have done, if she does not succeed in destroying me—then her brother will. I must roll with these crosscurrents of emotion and understanding of my situation. I must guard against the total loss of my heart.

Is it not baffling that each time I have loved it has been more intense, more real and consuming than the last? My love—yes, love—for Nina Hargrave makes my attachment to Jacqueline seem no more than a boyhood flirtation.

I have not written in this journal for several days. I have spent all possible time with Nina. We are together constantly. The guests in the inn now watch us with open curiosity and do not veil their gossiping behind raised palms and whispering. We ignore them. Nina in her brightly colored gowns and I wearing the joy of her presence, we chat and laugh through our dinners. When the sun is out, we spend our afternoons in the gardens or walking along the narrow streets and paths leading down to the sea. Should it rain, as it often does, we lock ourselves in her rooms, she sends Sarah away for the afternoon and we make love.

Almost—almost!—my mission is overshadowed. I can forget about Charles for hours on end. After such moments of freedom, however, the thought of him returns to haunt me and becomes an even heavier burden. I am thrown into dark moods and must beg leave of Nina to retire to my own rooms to struggle alone with the evil.

After each such bout with myself, I plague her with my doubts by demanding reassurance of her love. She gives it willingly, uncomplaining.

I have never known such sensual pleasure as that of which she is capable.

Today has been a black day. My happiness has been blotted out.

A letter from Charles Arledge has arrived. I found it shoved beneath my door when I returned to my chambers to change for dinner. As soon as I spotted the seal, my hands began to tremble.

> *My Dear André,*
>
> *My father has fallen ill and, according to his staff of doctors, will not recover. I find myself in an awkward position, having already become liable to my creditors for my share of the inheritance. It is most imperative that you proceed with the latter part of our plan at once.*
>
> *When I hear of your success, I will deposit ten thousand pounds in your name in Paris. I will also see that the original of your confession is returned for you to destroy with your own hands. Proceed with care—and haste.*
>
>

Affectionately,
Charles

The thinking part of my mind took time to absorb the letter—rejecting *the latter part of our plan.* How could I be the instrument to murder the woman I loved? Would I not rather take my own life? Or let Charles use my confession to bring ruin down upon me? Better ruin, better my own life than to kill Nina. But, I reasoned, if I refused, what of Sarah? Was she the second in this well-conceived plot of murder? What hold did Charles have upon her? She most certainly would not suffer the compunction that plagued me. How had she been instructed to act? A bit of poison in her mistress' tea? A gentle shove from the terrace?

I visualized my beloved writhing in the agony of poison. I saw her body—her exquisite body—twisted and lifeless on the garden stones beneath her terrace.

"Charles Arledge, you are a fiend!" I wept. "You are a monster to destroy good and beauty for the sake of an inheritance."

I cursed Charles. I cursed myself. I cursed even Jacqueline for the chain of events that had led to our unfortunate meeting.

When Nina stopped at my room to have me escort her to dinner, I was sitting slumped in my chair, a half-empty bottle of cognac on the table beside me, Charles's letter crumpled in my hand. In my drunken haze, I saw her glide almost dreamlike across the room and bend down beside my chair. There was concern in her eyes, fear, worry about the corners of her mouth. She touched my hand, the hand that clutched the letter demanding her hasty death.

"André," she whispered. "André, my love! What is it? Are you ill?"

She brushed her lips gently against my cheek, and the touch of her, the familiar smell of her fragrance brought tears to my eyes.

"Have I hurt you? Have I said something?" she pleaded.

I could not bear the fear for me in her voice. I willed my tears to cease. Dropping Charles's letter into the waste receptacle beside my chair, I rose and, taking her face in my hands, kissed her lips and eyes.

"I will never hurt you," I vowed. "You will never suffer at my hands."

Nina moved beneath me, demanding freedom. Sighing and wishing we could remain as we were and not face reality, I rolled away from her and lay watching as she rose and began to dress. How lonely it seemed without her quietly beating heart pressed beneath my head. How far away she seemed at only five paces.

"Aren't you dressing?" she asked, reminding me that I had promised to walk with her from the inn to the shore-line—a hearty walk for one in good spirits, but mine were at their lowest ebb. "Hurry," she said, "or we shall not be back before lunch."

I rose obediently, if weakly, and began to slip into my clothes.

"Ah, hunger makes you move," she laughed.

"Hunger indeed. We missed dinner and breakfast. If we do not take care, we will surely starve." I made as if too weak to continue to stand and fell back onto the bed mockingly. "My lady consumes me and refuses me nourishment. She is a heartless slave master."

But I could not jest with sincerity. Charles's letter was ever present in my mind, the words stamped there to taunt me through every hour. I abandoned any effort at humor, rose, dressed and reached for the cognac bottle. Nina, toying with her hair at the vanity, was watching me in the surface of her mirror.

"You promised not to become intoxicated again," she reminded me quietly. "I've told you how the smell of liquor repels me."

I drained the glass in one quick gulp despite her protest. "To steady my legs for the climb," I told her. "And I shall hide the sin of liquored breath by chewing tobacco."

Her gaze was steady. "What is wrong, André?"

"Nothing," I lied.

"Have you grown bored with me already?"

"Never!" I cried. "Never would I grow bored with you."

She laid her comb aside and, turning on her stool, met my gaze directly. "Then why do you make humorless jokes like a court jester trying to hide behind his mask?"

I turned away, saying nothing.

"I know you well enough to understand that something is troubling you," she said from behind me. "Do you not trust me enough to confide in me?"

"I would trust you with my life," I said.

"But not your troubles?"

I half-whispered, "There is something I must tell you. Something so terrible, so evil that telling you will be like sentencing myself."

"Sentencing yourself to what, André?"

"To life without you," I told her. "For once I have made my confession you will shun me like a leper . . . which is as it should be. I deserve no more."

"You are frightening me."

"I must."

"It is that you do not love me," she cried suddenly. "You have merely been entertaining yourself with my affections. Is that what you would confess?"

I crossed the room to her hurriedly, lifted her from the stool to her feet and held her into the curve of my trembling body. "If that were but true," I told her. "If I had but been playing with your love, I would do what I came here to do. Then I would go away and forget you. It is because I love you that I must make my confession. I must do it to protect you—even at the sacrifice of myself."

She disengaged herself from my embrace. Stepping back, she stared at me as if trying to see into the depths of my soul. "Then make your confession," she said coolly, and I thought that she had decided I was about to admit to being a fortune hunter or collector of women.

I stammered and searched for words. Finally, I said, "It concerns Charles, your brother, and myself."

I could see her body go tense. Her facial muscles appeared to become frozen, expressionless. When I made as if to reach for her, she stepped farther away from me. I was now someone to fear, a deceiver, at the very least, who was about to confess his deception. She walked away from me to the window and stood gazing sightlessly down into the courtyard. Her hair, ill pinned by her own hands, had come free and straggled about the nape of her slender neck. Her back was straight, her chin lifted like that of a man defying an opponent to strike him. Presently, as if laden by too heavy a burden, she slumped onto the window bench, folded her hands in her lap and turned her gaze back to my face. I could read nothing on that pale face, nothing in those cold blue eyes.

"You would confess to me of a conspiracy," she said softly. "My brother's name on your lips has left me weaker than the lack of food. How far I have traveled to escape him, and how near he now seems in you, whom I trusted more than any mortal man. What is this connection between you and my brother? What must you confess because of your love for me?"

How I wished to spare her what I must tell. But I could not. Her safety depended on her knowledge of her brother's intentions. She had to know how far he would go to destroy her. I went to her and seated myself beside her, and quietly, I began to tell her the story that had led to our meeting. I was merciless to myself; perhaps thinking myself a martyr to my love, I accepted the blame that was mine. I confessed my debauchery, my obsession with Jacqueline, my crime of murder. When I came to the part where Charles entered my life, her eyes glowed with strong interest. I thought that she would speak, but she did not. I meant her to listen, and she would not interrupt.

"You say the odor of liquor repels you," I finished. "If it had been so with me, I would never have drunkenly made a written confession and become your brother's pawn in this plot to take your life."

She continued to sit and stare at me with an unfathomable expression. Her hands were cold, but not trembling. I was aware of her pulse; it was steady, unhurried, as I would not have expected it to be. Only I, it seemed, had been affected by my confession. My voice had begun to crack before I had finished speaking, and I had been forced to struggle with my emotion to prevent myself from flinging myself at her feet to beg forgiveness.

Nina suddenly withdrew her hands from mine and got slowly to her feet. She crossed the room and removed her cape from the armoire, drew it about her shoulders and then turned to me. "Our walk," she said calmly. "I'm afraid we have already missed lunch." She walked out of the room, and I, baffled, thinking the strain of what I had told her had been too much for her, grabbed my coat and followed.

We took a winding path, made firm by decades of inn guests making their ways to the shoreline below. A wind had come up, and the sun had hidden itself behind threatening clouds. Nina's cape and skirts whipped about her legs, and her hair, torn completely free of its combs and pins, danced about her cold eyes and silent lips.

We did not speak until we had reached our destination. Exhausted and dizzy, I fell back to recoup my strength, while Nina moved ahead. She waded into the tide without noticing the cold. My first thought was that she had taken leave of her senses, that my confession had been too much for her to bear and that she intended to walk into the water until it claimed her. I ran forward, but without reason. She climbed suddenly onto the edge of a mound of rocks. She looked back at me an instant, a challenge in her gaze; then, clutching the jagged edges of the stones, she hoisted herself upward until she stood on their crest. The surf pounded about the base of the rocks and sent a spray over her. She did not cower and turn away, but lifted her face to receive it.

I removed my shoes and scampered after her, fearing she would fall and be killed among the rocks. What insanity had gripped her? I had expected tears, a rage, possibly even for her to faint, but I had not expected this behavior. Lifting myself to my feet beside her, I fought the wind for her cape and wrapped it about her shoulders.

"Nina! Come away!" I pleaded. "Come down before the waves pull us into the sea!"

But she did not obey me. She turned her wet face up to mine. "André," she cried against the din of the waves and wind. "André, do you truly love me?"

"I love you! I love you more than life itself!"

Her lips parted in a satisfied smile that lingered about the corners of her mouth. The smile, her wet hair clinging to her face—they gave her a strange appearance. I was filled with the same sense of foreboding I had sensed the morning I had approached her in the garden when she had clutched the bloodred book to her body and had reminded me of a black widow spider. I held her firmly and gently pulled her back from the edge of the rocks.

"André!" she cried. "What you must do should be obvious to you!"

"Come away," I repeated. "We will talk on shore!"

"No! Here, André, my love!" She reached up, clutched at my neck and bent my face down to her own. "Look into my eyes, André. See what it is that you must do."

I stared at her.

"You must go to London," she cried. "You must go and murder Charles!"

PART TWO

An hour from port we entered a thick fog, which has slowed our progress. All hands are on deck for the difficult entry, and I, having gone above to escape the confines of my cabin, found that the hive of activity only increased my nervousness. I have returned below to sit with my journal.

As I make this entry, I am consumed with loneliness. I am impatient to complete this foul task and return to Nina. She waits for me at the inn, guarded by Emile, who promised to protect her should Sarah return. The maid Charles chose should have been an actress. Her tears and pleas of innocence almost convinced me when her mistress dismissed her.

Charles, how well you chose my second, but how mistaken you were in me!

The ship's bells are announcing our arrival in port. I must close this entry in my journal and prepare to disembark. It will be near midnight when I reach the Arledge estate—a good time to search for the confession Charles must have hidden somewhere within his rooms. It is Saturday. Charles, unsuspecting of the irony of his fate, will be searching the taverns along the docks for a companion to satisfy his depravity. If he is true to form, he will not return home until near dawn or later. I will have to contend only with sleeping servants and a dying old man. Neither should much hinder my search. When my drunken confession is found and destroyed, then I shall do what I must to free both Nina and myself from her brother.

Charles, I wonder if you will die well.

The gatekeeper drowsed in his cubicle, his head against the window frame, his snoring shattering the late-night quietude. His dog, a shepherd of extraordinary size, took more interest in passersby. He got to his feet, examined me closely and, deciding I was no threat, lay down again with his head resting on his great paws. In the distance, I could see the enormous house. It was ghostlike in the moonlight, its cupolas rising as high as the tallest trees of the grove in which it nestled. There was a single light burning: in the entryway, I decided, where it would blaze until Charles returned home to extinguish it.

Pulling my head down into the collar of my greatcoat, I continued to walk about the wall, leaving the roadway and searching for the rear gate through which Charles had brought me in secret that fated night in the past.

I was surprised at my calmness; it could have been that I was accustomed to breaking into mansions, only generally through the front door at some social occasion. I did not fear discovery, only vaguely a tinge of discomfort to think of the gatekeeper's dog lunging for my throat. I had a knife in my pocket along with Nina's tiny pistol, but I doubted that either would be effective against such a creature.

The gate was grown over with ivy. I located the latch and put my shoulder against the rotting door. It swung slowly inward, giving off an alarming creaking sound. I froze, scarcely breathing as I waited, expecting the dog's barking to suddenly shatter the stillness and awaken the sleeping gatekeeper. After several moments, when the creaking had ceased to echo through my head and there was no sound of the shepherd, I wedged my body through the narrow opening and stood in the rear courtyard staring up at the moon-reflecting windows. I dug into my memory in order to orient myself. My basement room had been beneath the pantry; I had lain and listened to the servants' comings and goings. I had stared from my tiny square of a window into this very garden, better kept then than now. As to the heart of the great house itself, I knew nothing: only that Charles's rooms were on the second floor. How many others slept there? Had Nina's rooms been there? Was her father's? I suspected the old man would have been moved to the main floor in his illness, if not for his own sake then for the sake of the doctors and nurses.

I would have appreciated enough time to wander about the rooms that had been Nina's, to touch the belongings she had touched, to feel the vibrations of her that must linger about her favorite trinkets. I would have liked to select something of her own to carry away with me. Thoughts of my beloved spurred me on toward the scullery door.

A strong piece of wire worked easily enough on the door

latch. When the aged lock clicked open and the door was ajar, I stood in the frame and stared into the dimly lit, orderly room. Inside, my pulse began to quicken; perspiration beaded on my forehead. What time, I wondered, did the servants begin their day? I tried to remember, but I could not. Those days in the cramped basement room had been without an awareness of time, a limbo in which only Charles's visits had had meaning. I had three hours at the least before my presence would be risky—four hours at the outside. It was best not to waste a single moment. Because I knew Charles, knew that he was the sort of person who keeps everything closely about him, I was assured some drawer of his bureau or desk would reveal that which I sought. I had only to locate his rooms.

I felt my way down the darkened corridor, listening at each door before daring to open it. Eventually, when I thought I had become lost in the maze of doors and passages, I saw a thread of light from beneath a distant door. My hand was damp as I turned the cold metal knob and found myself peering into the lighted entryway. My eyes took in the furnishings, the crystal and wood paneling, the marble floors and winding staircase.

Nina passed through this entryway almost every day of her early life, I thought. Her eyes saw what I am seeing. Her feet crossed this floor and climbed those stairs; the railing remembers the touch of her hand.

I imagined I could hear her laughter still, her heels clicking across the marble as she returned from some past carriage ride or a day of shopping.

Heels clicking across the marble floor!

On tiptoe, I dashed across the entryway and up the staircase, taking care to step only on the inside edge of each stair so that a possible weakened board would not sound an alarm. The second-floor corridor did not enjoy any degree of moonlight; the surrounding trees outside gave a dull glow to the distant windows. I could make out shapes, a potted plant, a commode. I found what I judged to be the center of the corridor and moved slowly forward.

The first door yielded without sound, swinging open into a room with sheer white curtains and the shadowy form of a canopied bed: a lady's room—but not, I decided instinctively, Nina's. Perhaps it was her late mother's room. I pulled the door closed and moved on to the next.

After discovering two linen closets and a room, judging from its musty odor, not in use, I opened a door into a room and was instantly struck by the aroma of pipe tobacco, one of Charles's less-depraved vices. I stepped quickly inside and closed the door behind me. The draperies had been drawn against the night, and I found myself in complete darkness. I would have to risk a lamp, but first to locate one. I moved ahead; my leg struck a footstool, and it overturned with a thumping sound.

"What . . . who?"

A match flared, and before I could flee, a lamp blazed. An elderly man, his hair as white as the linen from which he raised himself, blinked under the glare with as much surprise as my own.

"Who the devil are you?" he demanded. The inflection in his voice, his blue eyes and familiar set of his mouth identified him instantly as the elder Arledge.

I stared at him, speechless. My fingers located and clamped about Nina's pistol. Lord Arledge did not have the appearance of a dying man.

"Char . . . Charles," I finally mumbled. "Charles said you were . . . were dying!"

The tension left his face. He lay back on his pillows and looked at me. "So you are a friend of my son's?"

I nodded.

"Well, he would have me dead, I grant you. But I will disappoint him for a time longer." The question of my presence in his room suddenly returned to his eyes.

He is wondering, I thought, if I have been sent to murder him in his sleep. My nerves calmed at my demand. "I went below," I lied. "Coming back to my room, I lost my way." I glanced down at my coat. "I could not sleep and planned to walk about the grounds."

The old man adjusted his position with considerable effort, reached for a glass of water from his bedside table and moistened his lips. "A man has various reasons for insomnia," he said. "It would be indiscreet of me to question yours. I suffer from the same malady. My reasons, like my age, are greater in number than yours could possibly be, young man. Still, I do not amble about the grounds past midnight." He sighed wearily. "I must look to my health. If a chill does not get me, the watchdog might." He chuckled to himself. "You see, friend of my son, I refuse to die until an heir has been born into this accursed family of mine."

As he wet his lips once again, I backed toward the door.

"Will you leave me now?" the old gentleman asked. "You awakened me, and now I shall not return to sleep easily." He motioned me back toward his bed. "Come. Spend a moment more of your time with me. I meet few of Charles's friends." He smiled. "I would actually care to meet fewer of them. But since we both suffer from the malady of insomnia, we have something in common, do we not?"

I reminded myself that this was Nina's father, the be-getter of her life. I had come to search his home, to murder his son. I owed him the debt of listening to his ramblings. I removed my coat and took the chair he nodded toward. When he asked for my name, I could think of none other than:

"Emile Favière, sir."

"A Frenchman?"

"Yes."

"You have the good looks of your nationality," he said.

My looks nowhere equaled the handsomeness of the man whose name I had stolen on impulse, not wishing to divulge my own.

"How do things go in your country? No, don't tell me. I have had my fill of the topic. Men talk of little else. Your writers, like ours, are forming a new kind of literature. I have read your Victor Hugo and Charles Nodier. I can read between their lines." He pulled himself up against the headboard and reached for his pipe, letting it dangle unlighted between his lips. "The English have a morbid fascination with the French. Do you know that an English firm is printing a book on the genius of Napoleon Bona-parte's campaigns? I find that ironic. We English are pe-culiar by definition. We threw off the Romans; we con-quered Philip of Spain; we protected ourselves against the navy of Bonaparte; yet we glorify these would-be conquerers of our country in verse and song and write little of our own bravery in comparison. Ah, but I said we would not talk of wars and heroes and the condition of your country. Tell me, Monsieur Favière, how did you come by friendship with my son?"

My mind searched and plucked out "In a card game, sir."

"Ah, yes," he said. "Charles has a knack with cards. Cards, unfortunately, are his greatest talent. I would have him turn his thoughts to marriage and a family, but he disobeys my wishes." His eyes became glazed with thought, his face set with resigned disappointment. "There, Monsieur, is a chief reason for my insomnia. I somehow find death, the idea of it, intolerable without the knowledge that the Arledge bloodline will continue. I have done my duty to God, country and ancestors, but time has weakened me. It is time for my son to relieve me of the burden, but he is stubborn and unreasonable. He would rather dally with cards and waste his seed in debauched pleasure."

I felt a sudden surge of compassion for this man. Perhaps my love for his daughter gave me insight into his desire for fulfillment through his children and grandchildren. I had had no children—I had not wanted them until now. I was still comparatively young. My death and the summing up of my life seemed far removed, but I was glancing, through Lord Arledge's eyes, at possibilities that might plague me in the future. Would Nina want children? We had not talked of it—or of marriage.

"But I should not talk of my son in this manner to you,"

the old man said. "You are his friend and loyal, and probably find me unreasonable."

"Perhaps," I said absently, "you should transfer your hopes to . . ."

"To? Please continue."

"Your daughter," I told him.

"My daughter? You have seen her on some past visit?" I told him I had.

He asked with a sudden uplifting of spirits, "Is she not a bewitching creature?"

"She is beautiful," I said meaningfully.

A spark flickered in his eyes, but it quickly died. "But she is a stranger to me," he said. "As strange in her way as Charles in his—perhaps even more so. I sometimes wonder if my late wife had insight when she cried that both our offspring had been born under evil signs." He lowered himself back down into his bed and drew the blankets about him. "Perhaps I shall die soon, as Charles wishes, as Nina is probably in accord with him. I shall escape the torment of them and find peace in the oblivion of my grave."

I shifted uncomfortably in my chair.

Lord Arledge closed his eyes. "You will find your room at the end of the hallway across from my son's, Monsieur Favière. Should you find yourself with an idle hour tomorrow, I would enjoy talking with you at length about your country. I have many questions concerning Bonaparte which might be answered by a Frenchman. Perhaps if I become obsessed with his genius as my compatriots have, I shall trouble myself less with my personal sorrows." He turned his head away from me.

"Good night, sir." I extinguished his lamp and crept back into the hallway.

Charles's room was locked, but the same piece of wire that had gained me my admittance into the house again succeeded. I lighted the lamp and stood wondering where to begin. The room held no less than four bureaus, an armoire, a desk and two giant commodes. In addition, there were numerous paintings behind which to hide a thing as compact as a piece of paper. I had had some practice at finding things hidden by Jacqueline, her favorite place being beneath the mattress, but that was too feminine and too common a hiding place for a man such as Charles. Besides, he was not reduced to changing his own linen; a maid would have discovered my confession immediately. I began with the desk—checking each drawer, carefully glancing through all notes and letters.

I met with failure.

The bureaus gave up nothing except silken undergarments, finely pressed shirts, cravats and stockings. I replaced each item as I had found it, feeling my impatience and fear grow with the passing minutes. I had wasted time with Lord Arledge. Charles, depending upon his success or failure, might return at any moment and discover me rifling his room. After convincing myself that the armoire contained nothing except clothing, I stood back in desperation and stared about the room. I noted that I had left two desk drawers ajar. I crossed to put them right—had my fingers on the handles—when my attention was caught by the intricate carving of the divisional slats. I tested them, applying pressure this way and that until I felt the carvings give. The slats slipped out and disclosed a secret niche. My heart leaped as I saw the folded sheet of paper. With trembling fingers, I unfolded the sheet and read my confession of murder.

I stuffed it into my pocket.

You have lost, Charles! You have lost your hold on me!

Better, I thought, to return the carvings to their places, leave things as I had found them. Why warn Charles? Why send him into hiding, suspecting my purpose for being in London instead of doing his bidding with his sister.

The carving jammed. Like an odd piece of a complicated puzzle, it refused to be fitted into place. I ran my hand into the niche and discovered a blocking item: a cold touch of metal. My pistol—the pistol I had bought in Paris and used to kill Jacqueline's lover! Charles had told me he had thrown it into the Thames.

I shoved it into my pocket, where it lay beside the confession and Nina's small pistol.

Glancing about the room to make certain I had left everything as it had been, I put out the lamp and came away content with myself for having succeeded in the first phase of my mission.

As I passed Lord Arledge's room on my way back down the corridor, I stopped, pressed my ear against the frame and heard his heavy breathing.

"Sleep well, old man," I whispered. "Soon you will need your strength to bury your son."

The clock in the downstairs entryway began to strike the hour.

"Five o'clock and all is well," I thought aloud.

Almost lighthearted, I descended the stairway and crept away from the house as I had entered.

Using a name which I no longer remember, I rented a room from an insolent-looking innkeeper near the docks. The fellow made it clear that for a price I could have whatever services struck my fancy—a tavern girl, or a woman with experience. I declined. No other woman could substitute for my Nina, not for a night or even a single hour.

I have not ventured from my room this day, considering it wiser not to tempt fate. I knew few people in London, only those I had met through Charles on past visits, but it would only take one chance meeting to involve me in the crime that I am to commit. I did not so much fear for my life as I did for a separation from my beloved. Should I be caught and imprisoned, I think I should consider suicide rather than the torment of separation; suicide, also, because I fear the agony of questioning might make me reveal her part in the crime.

No, no! I must not allow myself to think along these lines. Fate willing, I shall complete this nasty business with her brother and be with her again soon.

The weather brought an early darkness and a torrential rain that was driven along the streets by a backing wind. My hired coach, waiting inconspicuously in sight of the Arledge gate, had been parked beneath a gigantic tree for what precious little protection it afforded. The coachman, the collar of his mackintosh tucked under his hat, sat hunched over as if he had gone to sleep, his resignation to the weather matching that of his horses.

I was forced to keep my window down to prevent the pane from steaming. I did not trust the coachman's alertness in spotting the coach I had instructed him to follow. Leaning my head against the window frame, I felt the coldness of the rain against my face. I prayed the coolness I felt would be sustained through the ordeal of the night ahead of me.

It was perhaps an hour more before I heard the coach for which I had waited. It came quickly down the Arledge carriageway, paused momentarily at the gate, then sped into the street, turning in the direction of the wharf. I had no need to concern myself with the coachman's alertness. The sum I had promised him if he kept the coach in sight caused him to rouse himself. His whip snapped above the heads of the horses, and we joined in hasty pursuit.

When we came to an abrupt halt, I climbed down from the coach and found myself in the middle of Maritime Street, deserted now because of the weather. A few lights blazed in nearby inns, the sound of laughter occasionally reaching me during a lull in the wind.

The coachman leaned down from his perch. "The gentleman went into the Bonaventure," he informed me. "The inn and pub at the end of the block. It's a rough place, sir, for a gentleman. Will you be having me go in with you?"

I could see that the poor man probably doubted my return if I left him. "I'll manage alone," I said; and I paid the sum promised him and watched him out of sight.

Moving in against the buildings for protection against

the rain and wind, I walked slowly forward, my head brought down into the collar of my coat, my stride lacking haste but not determination. In my pocket, my pistol lay cold against my hand. This time when it had served its purpose, it would indeed be thrown into the Thames; I would see to it myself. I imagined the spirit of the pistol's first victim hovering about me. For one fearful instant, I considered circumstances that might confront me: the pistol refusing to fire at the crucial moment; my conscience preventing my pulling the trigger. Then Nina flashed into my mind—no, it was more than that: she seemed to appear before me, smiling, encouraging me—and all else vanished.

The Bonaventure was not crowded. There were perhaps half a dozen sailors and a table of local cronies slumped over their mugs—not enough clientele to keep the two serving girls occupied. They stood together, chattering and laughing. When they caught sight of Charles, both came forward to greet him. They conversed; then Charles, tipping his hat as chivalrously as to ladies of quality, left them and moved to the rear of the room. He disappeared through a door I suspected led to the rooms above.

Entering the inn, I selected a table near the rear door through which Charles had vanished. The girl who served me noted my hesitation to remove my rain-drenched coat, but she said nothing. I was obviously a foreigner, and she had been trained to ignore the peculiarities of Bonaventure patrons—especially the foreign ones such as myself who crowded the place during a ship's arrival. She brought me cognac and then retired a distance to resume her conversation with her companion.

None of the other patrons gave me more than a moment

of their attention; for that I was grateful. None would miss me when they noticed my table suddenly empty. I drank my cognac without apparent haste, savoring the warmth it brought to my throat and stomach. I had not eaten all day, and the cognac went directly into my bloodstream. I overcame the urge to order a second glass, and watching until I considered the moment advantageous, I rose and went quickly through the doorway taken by Charles.

I found myself at the base of a narrow staircase. It was dimly lighted, damp and musty, smelling of stale ale and decaying timbers. The first stair gave off a warning creak beneath the pressure of my weight, and remembering the stairs at the Arledge house, I pressed myself against the wall and ascended along the outermost edge.

The door on the upper landing opened onto a dank hallway which was also dimly lighted. The wallpaper, a flowery pattern, hung in shreds on the opposite wall, and the carpet at my feet was worn through the design. Here the odor of stale ale and decay mingled with that of human sweat and excrement. Charles, I thought, must truly have lost himself to his debauchery to hold a rendezvous in a place such as the Bonaventure. I closed the door to the stairwell quietly and crept forward, stopping at each room to press my ear against the wood.

From behind the third door, I heard muffled voices, distinctly male. I hesitated; concentration was required to recognize the voice of the man I sought. Bending to one knee, I pressed my eye to the keyhole and peered through, but without results. I could see only the tattered draperies on the opposite wall.

". . . reasonable," I heard Charles say. ". . . Only a

matter of time until . . . Then I can . . . without difficulty."

I could not hear enough to twist together the thread of their conversation, but from Charles's tone I understood the meeting was not what I had expected.

". . . a scheme that will ensure me . . . sole heir to both my father's and sister's . . ."

A second male voice sounded, low and deep-pitched and menacing. His reply came to me as a mere jumble of tones. I could recognize only the hostility behind his words.

I rose and glanced about the hallway. It would be necessary to conceal myself until the two men separated. If Charles left alone, as he had arrived, I would follow him. If his companion departed first, the room in which they met would suffice as a place of . . . of execution! But where to hide myself?

I could not wait in the pub below, nor did I imagine that any of the rooms had been left unlocked. The only place I discovered to conceal myself was the narrow landing outside the single window. I stared at it through the dirt- and rain-streaked glass. The platform was perhaps two feet wide, built in the days before the inn had been allowed to deteriorate to its present condition. The innkeeper's wife had most likely used it to support her flowerpots. One straggling plant remained—a weed, no doubt, which would drown in the storm. I would be forced to share its endurance of the elements; but I was already drenched, and it was a small price to pay for a hurried conclusion of my mission. Raising the window, I stepped carefully through and lowered it partway behind me.

The rain was cold, the wind causing it to find the space between my hat and collar. The wetness trickled down my spine. I dared shift my position only with the greatest care. The wooden structure had swayed beneath my first weight and threatened to collapse. Glancing nervously down, I found myself staring into a trash-filled alley which was lighted by the glow from the pub windows. I could imagine the jagged bits of bottles waiting to cushion my fall should the platform indeed give way beneath me. I clung to the outer frame of the window, and waited.

The wait was not a long one.

The door to the room opened and a burly man with a black beard stepped into the hallway. Standing in the bright light from the room he was leaving, he struggled into a heavy coat, talking over his shoulder as he dressed. He was a rough-looking fellow, the sort one avoids in public taverns. He glanced toward the window, perhaps feeling the draft, but he did not see my shadowy outline. His last words reached me clearly: "Until a week from to-day, Arledge! No longer!" He extended his bearlike hand, closed the door and made his exit down the stairwell.

I pulled up the window, climbed inside and moved quickly to the door. Before testing the lock, I placed one hand in the pocket of my coat and slipped my finger through the trigger of the pistol. My heart was pounding madly against my rib cage, and my hands trembled, I feared, almost too much to do my bidding.

"For Nina!" I whispered. "For our freedom!"

I wrapped my left hand about the door handle, took a deep breath and flung open the door.

Charles stood at the foot of the bed, slightly turned

away from the door. His shoulders were stooped, giving me the impression he was deep in thought. He was clutching the brass bed railing with such force his knuckles had gone white. Thinking, I suppose, that his companion had returned, he turned slowly.

"Now, listen, Whitman," he began. "I can't possibly raise that kind of money on such short . . . !" The words died in his throat when he saw me. His expression became one of puzzlement—then excitement. "André! Is it really you?" he cried.

I stared at him without speaking, thinking I should fire now. I should not allow him hope. I should not allow him to speak to me. I told myself to squeeze the trigger and let the bullet tear through my coat and into his body. But my hand would not obey; my finger remained lightly on the trigger.

Charles pulled himself erect. His face broadened into a smile. "You've come in person to tell me this damnable business is finished," he said. "It's good you've come. It's dangerous if you're seen with me, but . . . ! My friend, I have no cognac to offer you." I could see that his puzzlement was growing. He went on nervously, "You've done me a service. We must celebrate. Come, I'll go below for a bottle."

"No!"

He laughed hollowly, sensing, I believe, that all was as he feared. "What is this? André Laurent refusing cognac? Can this be?" He laughed again, but the laughter was even more forced.

I closed the door behind me, and he noted my use of my left hand. His eyes traveled to the bulge in my right pocket. The smile completely faded from his lips, and concern flickered in his eyes. His color paled, and his hand came back to grip the brass bedstead. His eyes darted about the room as if seeking an avenue of escape, then settled once again on my face. I had seen men as I was seeing Charles now—seen them on the battlefield when they had been trapped into facing death. I had also seen them in the surgeon's tent as they fought the inevitable conqueror of all men. I had seen them among Aleksandre Denisov's followers; yet these had had another aura about them; although some were maimed and diseased, there had still been some unexplainable hope in their eyes, as if they were expecting to be led away from the final blackness.

"Is Nina dead?" he asked in a wavering voice. "Have you killed her as you promised?"

"No, Charles. I have not," I told him.

Charles blinked a few times, as if suddenly bothered by a flash of light. Indeed, a light came, but it was behind him—a white flash of lightning that illuminated and filled the room. He flinched; he pulled back toward the window and away from me. There he stood motionless.

"Why are you here, André?" he asked in a low, incredulous voice.

"I think you know," I replied. "The irony of it should appeal to a man such as yourself, Charles." I turned the key in the lock in the event one of the waitresses should come to investigate his prolonged stay in the room above the tavern. "Of course, the irony would be better appreciated if viewed by an outsider." I pulled the pistol free of my pocket and aimed it at his heart.

"André, you can't!" he cried. "You can't kill me! Think, man! Think of all I've done for you, of all the times we had together. Didn't I risk prison and my own reputation to protect you? Didn't I hide you in my father's house until I could smuggle you back to France?"

"Yes, you did those things," I said calmly. "For your own purposes. You are as clever as you are evil. I did not understand you so well then."

He backed until he was pressed against the wall. There was a clap of thunder and he cowered, thinking it the explosion of my gun. His eyes widened, and I was struck suddenly by his resemblance to his sister. He had a curious masculine mixture of her beauty and style.

"Your confession," he stammered. "My God, man! Think of what they'll do to you when they find your confession!"

"They will not find it." I extended the pistol for him to see it more clearly.

The connection registered, and his hope crumbled. He whined and covered his face with his hands. This seizure passed quickly; then he pulled his hands away from his face and stared at me with open desperation.

"André, I beg of you!"

Although I did not wish it so, my smile must have been smug. "What would you have had me do if your sister had begged as you are begging now?" I asked him. "What would you have done to me if I had listened to her pleas? Would you have shown mercy, Charles? I somehow doubt it. I know it would not be so."

"I would! I would!" he assured me. "Because I am fond of you. André, you cannot be my murderer. You are also fond of me. I sense it! I know it! Why are you doing this for *her*? What has she promised you? What? More money? I will give it to you. I will give you double what she promised."

I felt the muscles of my stomach tighten. Why had I not just fired instantly and taken my leave? How would a man like Charles understand my reasons for doing his sister's bidding? The strongest affection he had felt was for himself.

He had taken my moments of distracted thought as a weakening. He came forward, back to the foot of the bed, and extended his hand to me. "I will give you half," he promised. "Half of two great fortunes. Think of it, André. Think of what luxuries such money could buy for you."

"I do not do this for money, Charles," I confessed.

"For what, then, pray tell?"

"For love."

"Love!"

"Of your sister!"

He stared at me in disbelief for an instant; then a remarkable thing happened to his face. The fear went from his eyes, his color returned, he even flushed. He threw back his head, and a laugh came from his throat by way of hell itself. When his laughter had died to an echo, he stared directly into my eyes.

"My friend," he said, "you have been played for a fool. You have been manipulated well. By an expert at such things. Did my sister promise to return this love of yours?"

"She *does* return my love!" I shouted at him.

What was this new expression on his face? Was it pity?

"You have made a grave error in judgment, my friend,"

he told me. "Nina is no more capable of love than I. Obsession, perhaps. But not the type of love for which a man kills. In that, we are two of a kind, my sister and I. We are of the same blood, from the same womb. Why do you think we have such contempt for each other? We understand each other."

"You are alike only in appearance," I argued.

"No, no, no! You have been blinded to her," he yelled. "Her soul is as dark as my own. No, darker. I admit to my wickedness. But where I am wicked, she is evil. *Evil*, André! You must see it."

I was seized by such anger that my entire body began to tremble. "It is you who are the evil one, Charles!" I cried. "And a fool besides to think you might save yourself by attacking her." I raised the pistol threateningly, but he no longer cowered. There was no fear in his eyes, only something vaguely resembling disbelief at his situation. It was he who would die, but I who trembled, shaken to the very core of my being by his accusations, his lies.

"Do you think her husband died naturally?" he asked. "And our mother? Did you not think it strange that a woman horrified of water should take her own life by walking into the sea? André . . . André! Admit you have been taken in! It is no crime. Her evil could blind the strongest of men! I have seen her turn men with wills of iron to putty with her . . ."

My pistol exploded, jerked and silenced his lies. There was a stunned expression on his face as the bullet tore into his chest; then he crumpled like a creature without a spine and lay in a heap on the dirty carpet.

The report of the pistol was immediately followed by

thunder. I stood without moving, waiting, fearing to hear doors opening, running footsteps coming to investigate. Moments passed slowly. Finally, convinced the sound of the pistol had been mistaken for thunder, I proceeded with what must be done.

I removed Charles's wallet and jewelry, transferring them to the pocket of my own coat. These I would give to Nina to prove I had succeeded in my mission.

We were now almost free.

Opening the door to the hallway, I peered about. There was no one in sight. I returned to struggle with Charles's body. Dragging it to the hall window where I had hidden, I opened the frame and pushed it through. It landed in the rubbish below with astounding quiet, taking with it the single flowerpot and the wooden ledge. I returned to the room, gathered up his hat and coat and threw them after him. Convinced nothing else had been left behind except the dark red stains on the carpet, I came away, descended the stairs and ordered a second cognac before leaving the inn and hurrying around to the alley.

Charles's body was heavy and awkward. I half-carried, half-dragged it down the alley away from the inn, stopping in doorways to rest, to wipe the rain and perspiration from my brow. I dared not glance at the dead face with its staring eyes. I tried to consider it nothing more than an unknown burden: waste to be disposed of in the dark waters of the river.

Concentrate on Nina, I thought. Think of nothing else. She is waiting for you! You can go to her soon. You are both free!

Her face appeared before me once again; her mysterious

blue eyes preceded me down the alley.

Voices reached me, and I froze, fear gripping me. Heaving the body, my burden, into a nearby doorway, I walked away from it toward the approaching men. There were two of them. They came down the alleyway from a warehouse, obviously intent on reaching the tavern. They stopped talking as they reached me and, I thought, were about to speak to me. I hunched myself over against the wind and quickened my pace to avoid being engaged in conversation. When they had passed me, I glanced at them over my shoulder and waited for them to pass the doorway with its silent occupant.

Not until I saw the sudden light from the distant door of the inn did I turn about and run to retrieve Charles's body. With the last remaining bit of my strength, I hoisted it onto my shoulders and hurried on to the end of the alley, where the cobblestones disappeared into the murky water. It slipped from my shoulders with a splash. Taking a pole, I poked and pushed it into the deeper water, watching it as it was caught by the current and drawn slowly away from the embankment.

My last sight of my victim was in a flash of lightning. The whiteness, the horror of those accusing eyes will live with me through the remaining days of my life.

Tomorrow, I sail. I return to my beloved. Perhaps with her I can forget.

I am haunted!

My physical condition mirrors the torment of my mind. Dark circles have appeared beneath my eyes, and my cheeks seemed to have been hollowed by lack of nourishment and sleep. The ship's captain has shown concern for me, not from interest but because I believe he fears the inconvenience of a passenger's death at sea. Since I cannot keep down my meals, he has instructed the cook to feed me on broths of herbs and goat's milk. He has sent me the ship's doctor, a coarse-looking man with shaking hands and an unsteady gaze, but I refused to be examined. What could he do for me? If I were religious, I should request a clergyman.

Tonight, before my dreams brought me from my bed to write in my journal, I dreamed of Nina. I dreamed of her soft, white body stretched out on a bed draped in deep red satin sheets. She slept untroubled, desirable, waiting to be awakened by the demands of my passion. I examined each curve and every contour of her body. I whispered my desire into her ear. Then, in my dream, my awareness grew. My mind's eye pulled back until I experienced the entire vision of the scene. I became both spectator and performer. I was kneeling beside her bed, naked, her slave, with my hands bound behind my back. I had no right to awaken her, no right to feel the desire surging through my body. I was but an instrument to be used at her discretion. Leaning my face against the red satin at her side, I inhaled the heady sweetness of her body, and my senses reeled.

As if sensing my nearness, my aggression, she opened her eyes and stared at me. I could see no love, no affection in those pale blue irises.

"I killed to free us," I whispered. "But I only succeeded in transferring my bondage."

She stretched out her hand and ran it through my hair as one might stroke a pet. A smile hovered about the corners of her mouth. "You complain without cause," she told me. "If it is your freedom you want, I give it to you. Go! Leave me!"

I was struck dumb, then found my voice to cry, "I cannot!"

"Then it could not be your freedom you seek," she answered. "Look to yourself, André. Did you not truly want to serve a master other than my brother? Did you not want to serve me?"

"I wanted to belong to you. I wanted to give you my heart—not my soul!"

She pulled me to her. "You have given me both," she said. Without the use of my hands, I could only submit to her demands. As she began to kiss and caress me, my sense of the spectator vanished. I was again within my own body, savoring her touch, her moist lips on mine. I closed my eyes and gave myself up to sensation.

"Nina, my beloved," I sighed.

But the hands grew more demanding. The caress turned into violent rage as our bodies collided. The kiss became a bite that drew blood. The sweetness of her odor turned foul; she smelled of decay and rotting flesh. I attempted to pull free, but was held firm. My eyes opened—and I screamed in terror.

Only inches from my face, unblinking, staring into my soul, were the blue eyes of another person: the lifeless eyes of Charles. Above my screams I heard the insane laughter of a madwoman—not Nina's, I told myself.

Charles's lips began to move. "She is evil. *Evil*, André," he moaned.

Terror climbed with me through the stages between nightmare and reality and brought me from bed with a leap, perspiration pouring from my body, my stomach knotted.

Surely these dreams will end when I am again with Nina. I could not survive if they did not. We dock day after tomorrow.

Nina—how happy I shall be when we are reunited.

It is late, sometime past midnight. The ship is tossing on a settling sea, the storm rumbling in the distance behind us. My eyes are heavy, my body weak from exhaustion. I must return to my bunk and hope for sleep. When it comes, I pray that I shall not be dragged back unguarded into Charles's waiting hands.

I arrived at the inn shortly after high noon. I was far too weary to acknowledge the proprietor's greeting, and I hurried to my rooms to remove my traveling clothes and shave the stubble from my chin before rushing to my beloved's side. Only my anticipation of seeing her again kept me from collapsing from exhaustion. I rang for Emile, but when he did not arrive, I proceeded to shave without him.

Minutes later, I was pounding on Nina's door, waiting impatiently for her new maid to answer the summons. When the door opened, I found myself staring at a gaunt, awkward-looking creature with a pinched mouth and colorless, squinted eyes. Surely, I thought, Emile could have found her a more suitable servant. She gave me a questioning stare and waited for me to state my business. My temper was short; I was in no mood to charm her.

"Tell Lady Hargrave André Laurent has returned," I instructed her.

She continued to stare at me, her mouth puckering over ill-fitted teeth.

"Tell your mistress I wish to see her," I repeated sternly. "Immediately!"

"My mistress," she answered, "is indisposed. Besides, sir, I think you have made an error. There is no . . ."

I pushed rudely past her and made for the familiar bedroom, with her cries of protest following me.

Confusion clouded my brain as I threw open the bedroom door and found myself intruding upon the toilette of a strange, misshapen woman. She stood before her vanity, sponging her obese body from a soapy basin. She spun about, screamed and attempted to conceal her nakedness with her arms and hands.

"Lady Hargrave!" I bellowed. "Where is she? Where is my beloved?"

My senses reeled; my legs, unable to support the weight of my body, gave way beneath me. Cries of protest from the lady and her maid rang in my ears. As the darkness claimed me, I remember the shattering of dislocated china as I pitched into the tea cart.

My beloved has gone!

The proprietor, after berating me for my behavior in the rooms of his new guest, informed me that Lady Hargrave had departed his inn the day after I sailed to England. She had given no excuse for the abrupt end of her stay; she had merely directed him to have her baggage transferred to a ship—he could not remember which ship— and she had paid her bill in full.

"Try to remember the ship," I pressed him.

He closed his eyes in thought. "If my memory does not fail me, Monsieur Laurent, the ship was named the *Capriccio*. Yes, that's it. I am sure of it. It flew an Italian flag."

The *Capriccio*: I repeated the name over in my mind.

I suddenly thought of Emile. He would know the reasons behind Nina's strange behavior. Maybe she had thought I would fail to kill Charles and had run to hide herself.

I instructed the proprietor, "Send me Emile."

"Emile, Monsieur Laurent?" he stammered.

"The valet," I said impatiently. I hoisted myself from my bed and poured a stiff cognac.

"Ah, Monsieur Laurent," the proprietor groaned. "That is another tragedy which has befallen my establishment during your absence. Emile proved himself a scoundrel. He has given my inn a bad name." He shook his head in disgust.

"I cannot sustain many more surprises," I told him. I returned to my bed and propped myself against the pillows. "Exactly what has Emile done to bring shame on your

143

inn?" I demanded. I saw his hesitancy and added, "And tell me the entire truth."

He continued to shake his head from side to side as if memory of some incident were best forgotten. But when he saw I would not be put off, he finally confided: "Emile made improper advances toward the lady. It happened the night you left us, but it is as if it were only yesterday. Youths today are alarming. You trust them, you give them employment, and they betray you."

"So you dismissed him?" I prompted when he fell silent.

"Dismissed?" he echoed. "Oh, no, Monsieur Laurent. It was not necessary to dismiss him." He leaned forward as if to impart a secret. "The lady shot him." He sighed and slapped his leg in a puzzling gesture.

"Emile was killed?"

"Oh, no, not killed. She shot him in the leg. A bad wound, too, I am told. The police came. The lady filed a charge, and Emile was taken away. We shall not be seeing him for a long while to come, Monsieur."

I told myself I should not concern myself with Emile's hapless fate. My mind had not room for more than Nina. I all but obliterated the proprietor's presence from my mind when the thought of her returned to plague me. Only by chance did I catch a scattered fragment of his rambling.

". . . but the English lady said it was not Emile's behavior that was driving her away. She would not tell me her reasons, although I pressed her. I had thought to encourage foreign trade by advertising in various newspapers, but now I fear the gossip of this incident, along with that of the strange death of that child, will ruin my fine plan."

I sat upright. "English lady," I said. "Are you telling me the lady Emile accosted was Lady Hargrave?"

"Yes, the lady of your acquaintance," he answered. "I thought you understood that."

"My God!" I cried. "She should have shot the bastard through the heart!" I had left Emile to protect her; unfortunately, I had left no one to protect her against Emile. Still, that did not explain her disappearance, her neglect to leave me a note or explanation.

"It would have been better for Emile also, I fear," the proprietor said. He rose and moved to the door. "Should you wish dinner served in your room, Monsieur Laurent, I shall be happy to oblige. Your absence from the dining room will give me an opportunity to relate to the Countess Mignot some story about the strain of your journey, your mistaking her rooms for those of another. Of course, she has most likely heard the rumors about the last quest in her rooms and will draw her own conclusions."

"To hell with her conclusions!" I cried.

Alone, I dropped quickly into the depths of despair. Even now, when it is nearing morning, the despair stays with me without promise of diminishing.

Nina—have you gone away to punish me for my original intent toward you? Were you using me as your brother used me? Was I but an instrument to you, a human boomerang which you cleverly turned to your advantage?

I must know the answers to these questions, and there is only one who might possibly supply them.

My finances are drastically low. I have only the money taken from Charles's wallet, less than fifty pounds, and my room rent to be paid. Tomorrow, I shall sell Charles's jewelry, my silver-tipped walking stick and my gold snuff-box. If the need arises, I shall even sell my wardrobe.

I must have money if I am to search for Nina!

PART THREE

The house to which I was directed stood on the side of a densely populated hill and looked, as had been suggested to me, as if it were at odds with the neighboring structures. While all the others houses faced east, this house faced southeast, its defiant angle affording the occupants the most advantageous view of the sea. The design was strictly modern; the owners obviously wealthy, and foreign.

I walked about the side of the house and approached the servants' entrance. Through the window I could see two women who were busy with the preparation of the noonday meal. The elder of the two answered my knock. She stared at me questioningly and with more than a little impatience.

I smiled, and said, "I'm seeking Miss Sarah Alberts. I was told she was employed in this household."

"She has been," the woman answered shortly. "Though there were plenty of French girls who could have done her job better."

"Of that I have no doubt," I said assuredly. "Could you ask Miss Alberts if I might have a moment of her time?"

The housekeeper cocked her head to one side; her suspicions grew. Why, she was asking herself, would a gentleman—a French gentleman—be wanting to chat with an English tart? "Miss Alberts," she finally said with heavy sarcasm, "is not receiving visitors." Then, with more authority, she added firmly, "She has her duties."

"And I shall keep her not more than is absolutely necessary," I said hurriedly. "It is a matter of some importance." I too could show authority. "I should hate to disturb your mistress. I have no doubt she would grant me the audience. Although"—I narrowed my eyes—"I have no desire to inform her I was denied a proper request to see her maid on business." I shrugged my shoulders and turned as if to take my leave.

"Wait, Monsieur," she said from behind me. "If it is business, I shall call her." She hesitated, not wishing to surrender her authority without a final remark. "See that you do not keep her long." She nodded toward a bench in the tiny garden. "You may wait there." Turning, she instructed the younger woman to summon the English maid, adding in a lower tone which I was meant to overhear, "I hope her Ladyship does not expect to receive her admirers on a frequent basis."

I retired to the bench, and waited.

It had been only by chance that I had learned from the proprietor of the inn that Sarah had not returned to England after Lady Hargrave had dismissed her. The pathetic creature, he had told me, came daily to the inn to ask about a possible letter from London. She had told him it was of considerable importance to her, and he had surmised that she had been expecting money. She had told him that she had taken a temporary position with English expatriates. Since the number of English families was limited, it had not been difficult to trace her, but what I hoped to learn from her was uncertain.

Sarah came to the kitchen door. When she saw me, she seemed about to turn and flee, but the housekeeper spoke to her with hostility, berating her for disrupting their morning schedule, and with a defiant toss of her head, she stepped into the garden and approached me timidly.

I stood and suggested she seat herself, but she would not.

"I haven't the time or inclination," she told me flatly.

I had witnessed her dismissal, and she had not forgotten my attitude of self-satisfaction.

"What possible business could you have with me?" she asked. "If you bring me more troubles, I don't need them."

I seated myself and met her eyes, hoping mine would convey the proper amount of sincerity as I said, "I have reason to believe that you have been wronged, Sarah."

She flinched slightly, cast her eyes downward and said nothing.

"I only learned by accident that you had not returned to London. I am surprised that you are still here."

"No more surprised than I, sir," she said. "I should not be if I had not, as you said, been wronged."

"By your mistress?" I pressed.

"Yes, by her. But also by her brother," she answered.

I felt my flesh prickle at a sudden image of Charles. "Will you explain?" I asked.

"Why should I?" Her stubbornness, which I had thought to be fading, flared once again.

"Because I might be able to help you," I told her.

"You!" She laughed uncertainly, and I knew in that instant she was beside herself, distressed to the point of hysteria. Her eyes filled to overflowing; her lower lip trembled. "Why should you help me?"

"We can call it an exchange," I said quietly.

"An exchange?"

I again had the impression she was about to turn and flee.

"Sarah, I also have been wronged. By both your former mistress and her brother. I shall not explain the circumstances, although I have the suspicion you may already be aware of them, but . . ." I stopped in mid-sentence, staring into her eyes to judge her reaction to the implication.

She was sharp enough to understand my probing gaze. She met it directly and said, "I am not aware, Monsieur Laurent, of anything except my own circumstances. I am stranded in a foreign country, in a hostile household, because I was dismissed from my position for some unknown cause and because Charles Arledge, deceitful man that he is, has ignored my plea for a return passage to England." Her voice had grown louder as she spoke, raised in anger at the injustice done her, and the housekeeper was drawn to the doorway to listen.

"You are indeed in a predicament," I said sympathetically. "But how can you protest your innocence where your mistress was concerned? Were you not in the employ of her brother?"

"Aye, I was. But she must have been aware of it from the beginning. It was her brother who sent me to her for the interview. I did my work. What more could she have wanted?" Her eyes blazed. "And I closed my eyes to everything that was no concern of mine."

I concealed my surprise over Nina's knowing the servant came from her brother. If she had known the maid had been recommended by Charles, why had she seemed so perturbed when I had told her my suspicions that Sarah was reporting her every move? Had the spy been sent to see that I carried out my black deed? "What exactly were your instructions from Charles Arledge?" I asked.

She looked at me a moment without answering, perhaps wondering if she should betray Charles's trust by replying. The letter with her return passage might still be coming. She was weighing my help against that of Charles. To her knowledge, I was also rich. I could give her the money for passage; I could be her avenue of escape from the hostile woman in the doorway, from this country of French barbarians which she did not like or understand.

"I told it all to Emile the night you left," she finally told me. "I went to him at the inn. I told him I had been wronged, that I did not understand Lady Hargrave's reasoning in doing something so terrible to me as to cast me out without enough money to return home."

"And Emile said he would approach Lady Hargrave?" I suggested, visualizing the gallant Emile coming to her rescue like a true Frenchman.

"Aye," she said. "And look where it got him. He is in more trouble even than I." She lowered her head, and a sob broke from her throat. "She said that he attacked her, and she shot him." Lifting the hem of her apron, she dabbed at her eyes. "I should have gone directly to the lady to plead my case," she moaned. "But I was afraid of her—truly afraid. It was a foul day that I came to Lady Hargrave."

"A foul day for both of us, I fear," I said with a heavy heart.

The housekeeper did not like it that we had lowered our voices. She had hoped for a choice bit of kitchen gossip to make the English maid's life more miserable. She glared at us openly.

"Why were you afraid of your mistress?" I asked.

As if the memory caused her fear to return and weakened her legs, she sat beside me. "I cannot answer," she said.

"Cannot, or will not?" I demanded.

"Sir . . . Monsieur, I am still afraid," she sobbed.

"Afraid even to tell me? I offered to be your friend and help you if I could, yet still you hold back from me." I shook my head as if injured by her lack of confidence.

"She was . . . was strange," she said shakily. "She had strange ways and did strange things."

"What do you mean?" I pressed. "Tell me, Sarah, please."

"There were many things strange about her. I cannot give you a single one that will make you understand my fear of her. It was mostly little things, odd things she did when she thought I was not about."

I prompted her with my eyes.

"At night," she said. "Very late at night, she would rise from bed, if she had retired. I would hear her singing—no, chanting softly, in a deep-throated tone."

"Probably praying," I said. "I have heard it is a custom with some sects."

Sarah glanced at me, then quickly lowered her gaze. "None I'd ever heard of," she said. "I asked myself to whom she was praying." A shudder passed through her body, and she clasped her hands together as if to stop their trembling. "And her late-night wanderings," she said. "I would hear her rise and dress and leave her rooms, sometimes not to return until near dawn."

"Where did she go?" I asked, shaken by her information.

"I never knew," Sarah confided. "But one morning she returned with blood across the front of her cloak. She had tried to wash it away, but had not succeeded. A lady such as herself seldom knows the secrets of such domestic handiwork. I knew she did not want me to see it—she had folded the cloak and stuffed it into a trunk. I left it there. It was the morning of the news of that poor child, the one who was found sacrificed by some demon."

It was my time to shudder. I tried to conceal it, but Sarah was attentive and nodded knowingly.

"It frightened me, sir—of that you can be sure. I wanted to be free of her, but I was afraid to give notice. What was I to do? Then her brother would most certainly not have sent me my passage. Had it not been for being stranded in this godforsaken—pardon me, Monsieur Laurent—if it had not been for being stranded in your country, I would have quit then and there and considered myself fortunate to be free of her. Later, when she dismissed me, I was both relieved and frightened of the fate that had indeed befallen me." She met my gaze and added with conviction, "But I was not guilty of any disservice. There was no cause for my dismissal."

"I believe in your innocence," I told her. "Please tell me your exact instructions from Lady Hargrave's brother when he obtained the position for you with his sister. And let me warn you, Sarah, I will know if you are lying to me."

"I do not lie, sir," she assured me with dignity. "I was told I must keep a protective eye on the lady. Her brother said I was to be particularly wary of . . . of Frenchmen, who were all adventurers and fortune hunters." She cast down her eyes in embarrassment.

"Go on," I urged.

"He also gave me a letter," she continued. "He told me it was a warning to any man who would take advantage of his sister. Should any Frenchman become too attached to her, I was to slip the letter to him."

"And you delivered that letter to me?"

"Yes," she confessed. "I put it under your door."

Charles's letter informing me of his father's illness and instructing me to proceed with the latter part of his plan with haste—with Nina's murder.

Charles's cleverness exceeded my original concession. Not only had he understood his sister's desirability; he had also anticipated my weakness, my surrender to her wiles. He had devised the scheme of the letter to inter- cept, to prevent these possibilities, but Sarah, because of timidity or lack of immediate perception, had delivered the letter too late. I had already been trapped.

"Is that all of it?" I asked.

"It is," she assured me. "Except if the letter failed, I was to write to him without delay."

"Did you write to him?"

"No," she said weakly. "Not about his sister's affair with you. I knew it was too late to stop it, and I did not want to bring trouble down on myself—or my mistress." Her eyes blazed with renewed anger. "I should have been of a different mind," she said. "I was thoughtful of her and treated badly for it."

"Indeed you were," I agreed, hoping to fan her anger.

"And you, Monsieur Laurent? How were you wronged?"

Not that I did not have the desire to confess to her, to confess to anyone to unburden myself, but I could not; I must carry my betrayal in secret, if only to protect myself. "In my heart," I said with a dramatically painful lilt.

She accepted my explanation with the ease one would expect of such a woman. She moved closer to me and was about, I thought, to take my hand to comfort me. "She is what my good mother would have called an evil slut," she said, and her voice, carrying to the doorway, sparked the housekeeper's waning interest.

I assumed a brooding expression. "If I learned everything possible about her, perhaps I could end this obsession." I meant to draw out more from Sarah.

But she gazed off with half-sight and said, "I have told you all I know, Monsieur Laurent. If I knew more, I would tell you. I know there was someone she saw besides yourself, but I don't know who."

Something tightened within my chest. I mumbled aloud, "Could this be true?"

"I would swear by it," Sarah said.

The housekeeper cleared her throat and stepped into the garden—a signal that enough time had been wasted.

Sarah got to her feet. "I am sorry I am not able to help you more," she said honestly. "But I cannot even help myself. I am in bondage to this household until I can save enough money to book passage home." Her voice was tinged with pleading, with hope that I might become her benefactor.

I stared up at her, thinking she was far less unattractive than I had originally labeled her. She was open, honest. Despite her own problem, there was genuine sympathy in her soul for me. Reaching into my pocket, I extracted my wallet, fat with the proceeds from the sale of Charles's jewelry and my own few precious items. I counted out enough bills to buy her a second-class passage back to England and pressed them into her hand.

"God bless you!" she cried. She bent and kissed my cheek; then, turning, she fled across the yard and through the kitchen door, almost upsetting the housekeeper, who refused to relinquish her space in the frame.

God bless you! she had said.

I felt I would need every blessing that could be given me.

The *Capriccio* was bound for Palermo.

There is a ship leaving tomorrow for Leghorn in Italy. There, I am told, I will most assuredly find passage to Palermo. I will soon be in pursuit of *my* Nina.

This morning after visiting Sarah, I returned to the inn and packed my belongings. In the trunk I had brought on my return from London, I discovered the topcoat I had worn that last night. The lapel and left shoulder are stained and matted with dried blood. Nina's toy of a weapon and my own pistol, which in my excitement and haste I had neglected to throw into the Thames, were still nestled in the pocket. I wrapped Nina's weapon in a handkerchief I had stolen from her bureau as a memento and packed it in my trunk; my own pistol I will now carry.

This afternoon I shall visit the city's bastille. Perhaps Emile will be capable of shedding more light on the mystery Nina.

A few francs placed in the hands of the jailer quieted his objections to my visiting a prisoner. A stout, offensive man in his late forties with gray hair and black, cold eyes, he wore his uniform with the arrogance of assumed superiority. His brass buttons were shiny, new, sewn onto a fading jacket by feminine hands. There was a scar on his left cheek and another on the knuckles of his right hand. His nose had been broken and had not been reset, giving his face more the look of a criminal's than that of a keeper's.

He counted the francs and then shoved them into the pocket of his jacket. Seating himself behind his desk, he leaned back in his chair and used his cold, dark eyes to turn a gaze on me meant to frighten me and send me scurrying through the door with my request for visiting privileges forgotten. When he saw that I was not intimidated and met his gaze with a coolness of my own, he rose, sending his chair grating across the floor with a push from his legs. He unhooked the keys from his belt, and I followed him through a heavy door, down stone steps and into the odorous passage between two rows of cells.

"We have had strange happenings here," the jailer suddenly informed me. He stopped and, blocking the passage, turned, an odd expression on his face. "Only recently," he said—and shook his head as if even now disbelieving what he was determined to relate—"when the guards made their morning check of the cells, they found one that had housed some forty prisoners empty. Empty!" he repeated as if I had not comprehended his statement. "Ah, but even stranger was the manner in which the prisoners escaped." He lifted his hat and scratched at his head with his index finger. "A complete section of the cell wall was missing. It looked as if some intense blaze had burned an opening directly through the bricks and mortar." He proceeded a few steps and then stopped again. "Of course, all were caught—except one."

I don't know what prompted me, but I asked, "Was that one Aleksandre Denisov, the mystic?"

"*Oui!*" he said. "Then the news has spread, regardless of our attempt to quiet it." He continued, mumbling, "A mystery . . . Where could a flame so intense come from? . . . And why did it not burn the entire prison? . . . Strange indeed!"

The cells were large, each housing more than a dozen prisoners. They were without the meagerest furnishings, the prisoners squatting on the stone floors or standing idly against the bars or slimy walls. In the center of each cubicle a round pit had been built into the floor; these, I noticed with disgust, served as toilets, a stench rising from them that defied description. There were tiny windows along the border of the ceiling, each scarcely large enough to accommodate the head of a grown man. They were not barred or fitted with glass, and the wind howled through them, chilling the stones and leaving the interior colder than the outside.

The jailer stopped before the fourth cell. Turning to me, he misread my disgust for fear, and smiled openly. He was experiencing a satisfaction I longed to destroy, but I said nothing.

"Favière!" he bellowed through the bars of the cell. "Emile Favière! Come forward!"

The prisoners became exceedingly stilled.

I searched their faces, but did not see my ill-fated valet.

"Emile Favière!" the jailer repeated in a shout.

None of the prisoners stirred.

"Your friend," the jailer said, "either has had his throat cut or has died in his sleep." He turned as if to lead me away.

I stepped forward and grabbed the bars. "Emile! For God's sake, it's André!" This particular cell was overcrowded. I turned from one passive face to another. "Do any of you know him? I am his friend."

"Prisoners have no friends," the jailer said from behind me. I could not see his face, but I knew that he was laughing—laughing at their misery and my ineffectual plea.

Then, as I was about to turn away defeated, the prisoners stepped soundlessly aside, and a man came through their midst from the rear of the cell. He was tall, thin, with a gaunt face. His clothes were in shreds, testimony to his long-term sentence. Although he was unknown to me, there was something vaguely familiar in those unblinking eyes. Before he had spoken, I told myself that I had seen that look in the eyes of Aleksandre Denisov's followers.

"Your friend," he said flatly, "is there." He tossed his

head to indicate the rear of the cell, where I could make out a shadowy form on the floor.

I felt myself sicken. "Is he dead?" I asked.

"He will be dead before next morning unless his leg is amputated," he said with the same lack of emotion. "He has gangrene."

Even when I had been in the army with soldiers dying all about me, the diagnosis of *gangrene* had always given me a chill. I had loathed to assist any surgeon in the removal of a gangrenous limb. There is no smell more straight from hell.

I felt myself anger toward this stranger for his lack of emotion over Emile's condition. He could have been telling me about the weather or giving me directions. I spun about to the jailer and vented my anger there. "Haven't you a physician to look after my friend?" I cried.

He had been listening with idle curiosity. He shook his head. "None will go in among them," he said in a tone that stated he agreed with them.

"Then he will just be left to die?" I cried incredulously.

"If God is willing," the jailer said with a shrug. "Your friend is now in His hands."

The prisoner who had spoken to me broke into a guttural laugh. The cruel lines about his mouth froze as I turned to him. His voice was still unfeeling as he said, "I have done what I could. I asked for instruments to do what must be done, but they were refused me."

The jailer backed from me when I turned my anger upon him again. He was no doubt wishing he had not accepted my bribe. He would have liked to be done with me so he might slip back into his ease of unconcern.

"I am not a man without influence," I told him threateningly. "I will not allow my friend to die without an attempt to save him."

"I could not put such instruments into the hands of a criminal," he told me. "This man is a murderer. He is here for killing two men in a brawl."

"Then bring the instruments to me," I told him. "I will be responsible."

He stared at me, bewildered by my demand. Yet my attitude challenged his authority and had pierced his bravado.

I could not allow him the opportunity to regain his composure. Stepping to the door of the cell, I ordered him to admit me.

"Monsieur," he said in disbelief, "you are either a very brave man or a fool. There are men in there who would kill you for the warmth of your clothes. Look at these scars." He pointed to the scars on his cheek and knuckles, then to his misshapen nose. "I narrowly escaped with these injuries—and my life."

"It is I who am taking the risk," I said strongly. "Admit me!"

He obliged with reluctance.

"And bring me the instruments this man requested," I said from inside the cell.

I am not a brave man—or a fool—but I have a sense of justice. My heart was pounding against my rib cage, my temples throbbing with fear. I stood uncertainly, trying not to consider my fate.

The gaunt-faced prisoner stepped forward. "They will not harm you," he said with confidence. "The jailer is a different matter. He is a cruel man who delights in their discomforts and misfortunes."

I contented myself with his assurance. He seemed to be their ringleader and seemed the sort to expect obedience from the other prisoners. He moved ahead, and the prisoners cleared a path for us.

Bending beside Emile, I took his head in my hands and turned his face into the dim light. I was seized by a pity so strong that I feared I would collapse and show myself as a weakling. I knew that if this happened, I would be lost. I would be killed and my body picked clear of everything save my flesh. The handsomeness had been drawn from Emile's face. His forehead was creased with pain, grime crusted in the crevices as evidence of considerable time in this condition. His eyes fluttered open; he stared at me unseeing, his sight glazed by delirium.

He grasped my arm weakly. "Mercy," he groaned. "Kill me!"

"He has been begging for death for days but still hangs on," one of the prisoners said from behind me.

I bit my lip. "Emile, it is André," I told him. "We will try to help you. I promise you we will do what we can."

He blinked several times in an effort to clear his vision. Weakly, he tried to lift his head from my hands.

"Lie back," I coaxed. Removing my coat, I folded it beneath his head.

His consciousness faded for a moment and then returned. "Lady . . . Hargrave . . . ," he mumbled. "Must . . . warn you, André . . . she is . . . is a she-devil." He cried out with a surge of pain. Tears formed in his eyes and overflowed onto his cheeks.

"Don't talk," I urged him, although I wanted desperately to hear what he had to say.

"Must . . . must talk," he stammered. "We . . . we were wrong about . . . her."

"I know, I know," I moaned.

In a voice scarcely audible, he said, "You do not know . . . how wrong. She belongs to . . . to no . . . man." Then his eyes closed and his body went suddenly limp.

I laid my hand on his chest and discovered he still lived.

The ringleader knelt beside me. He lifted the rags covering Emile's leg and showed me its condition. I hesitate to describe it—no, I will not. Even now, in the comfort of my room, I feel the sickness of my stomach rise up into my throat.

The prisoner touched my arm. His cold stare sought my eyes and judged my strength. "My name is Hugo," he said. "Perhaps I should do this thing." He hesitated before adding, "But you must assist me."

I steadied myself and told him I had done it before, on the battlefield. "Only then I did not know the patients," I added.

Hugo's lips curled away from his jagged teeth in understanding of my queasiness. "Tell yourself he is a stranger," he said. "A steer to be slaughtered for meat." The unnatural humor left his face. "Did you know him well, this youth?"

I nodded. "I feel responsible. Guilty. If it had not been for me, he would not be suffering as he is."

Hugo looked away from my face. "At least," he said, "you are man enough to admit it."

The jailer returned with several instruments tied into a

sheet. He called me to the cell door. This time he was accompanied by four armed soldiers, each with his rifle drawn and aimed into the cell. The fellow was, I thought, surprised to find me alive when he returned. He nodded toward the soldiers. "They were meant to avenge you," he said. He opened the cell door and passed the sheet through.

"We will need a fire to cauterize the wound," I told him. "And boiling water."

He nodded, seemingly caught up in the incident. He instructed one of his soldiers to bring the things I requested, and I returned to Hugo with the sheet and spread out the instruments for his inspection.

He examined each, weighing the scalpel between his fingers as if it were a weapon to be used in battle. "They will do," he said. He positioned the blade to cut through the outer, rotten flesh.

"May God guide your hand," I told him.

He flinched at my words. His eyes turned to me, cold and critical. "I have recently been taught by one who has left us to call upon other powers," he said. "Leave your god unsummoned. He will not work through my hands."

When the scalpel cut into Emile's flesh, he began to rise through his unconsciousness. His body began to twist and writhe, to rebel and protest the loss of his limb. Two prisoners, without being asked, stepped forward, one clasping his arms and the other his good leg. Hugo accepted their contribution as if they were practiced medics. Although the perspiration on his forehead seemed to belie it, he handled the scalpel with the precision of a surgeon.

There was cognac in the coat beneath Emile's head. I

snatched the coat away, dug into the pocket and withdrew the flask, forcing the liquor between Emile's parted lips.

"It's wasting good liquor on a man who will soon die," one of the prisoners said, but Hugo's glare silenced him from protesting further.

I was forced to turn away when Hugo exchanged the scalpel for a saw to cut through the bone; the sound of that splintering still echoes through my brain. That and the smell of seared flesh will stay with me forever, stamped eternally on my memory with the image of Charles's staring lifeless eyes—and Nina's face.

I felt my tension lessen only after Hugo had said, "It is done." He heaved a great sigh and dropped the instruments back onto the now-bloodied sheet.

I stared at Emile. All color had drained from his face. He appeared dead. The rags had been drawn back over his body; the absence of folds where his leg would have been struck me with renewed horror. Again, I felt responsibility, and was seized by remorse.

Emile had become another human being touched by the chain of evil that seemed to surround me. It seemed all the more pathetic in Emile because I had prophesied such great possibilities for him should he have learned from others' lessons. Jacqueline's English lover . . . Charles . . . Sarah . . . now Emile! If none had met me, how much would their lives have been changed?

"*Mon Dieu*," I whispered. "Where will it all end?"

I became aware again of Hugo's stare. Not once, but twice I had mentioned a god he rejected—one that even I had never called upon in the past.

The exhausted prisoner sat back on his haunches and continued to stare at me. "The English lady he spoke of," he said. "Is she the one who shot him?"

"She is," I said without hesitation.

"Then why do you blame yourself?"

"I cannot explain," I told him.

He seemed to accept this without question, although he deserved to know as much as I myself. He brought up his knees, rested his arms across them and leaned his head forward, his eyes fixed on mine from above the grimy sleeve of his blouse. "He spoke of her often in his delirium," he said quietly. "Depending on what pain-drugged fantasies seized him, he called her A Lady of Quality, The Foreigner or Creature of the Devil."

When he lapsed into silence, I pressed him by asking, "Did he say more?"

He nodded. "But who is to say what is true and what is not? I remember a man of my acquaintance in the war who swore his wife was a witch who changed sex at will. To him, it was undoubtedly a reality of his delirium, but I knew his wife and there was no more pious a creature."

The jailer, aware that the operation had been completed, was yelling for me to leave the cell. Ignoring his cries, I asked the prisoner, "What more did he say in his ramblings?"

"Is this lady your wife?" he asked.

"No."

"What then?"

"My . . . mistress," I mumbled.

He laughed hollowly. "Not," he said, "according to your

168

young friend. She is the slut of any man, but the mistress to the Devil himself!"

My jaw sagged. "That is surely to be attributed to his delirium," I managed.

A groan drew our attention to Emile. He stared at me, his eyes blinking as he fought back the pain. When the lids stilled, I saw that his gaze was not glazed, that he was in the midst of one of those rare moments that follow extreme agony in which the senses are perfectly sharp. His lips quivered.

"André," he uttered between clenched teeth. "I am not delirious now. The whore belongs to . . . to the mystic! She carries his child!"

I was stunned beyond speech. A scream tore its way from somewhere deep within my bowels. I leaped to my feet and would have driven my boot into the youth's face if Hugo had not grabbed me and dragged me to the door of the cell. Even as the jailer and his soldiers wrestled me up the stairs, I continued to bellow like a madman.

Nina, what crypt of Hell cracked open and allowed you to escape?

A flushed and breathless Sarah ran up to me as I prepared to board my ship. She was dressed unlike herself, in a gown meant for spring, pinks and whites, with a dainty lace collar and ruffled cuffs—a dress, no doubt, she had saved for a special occasion, costing less than her mistress' petticoat but more than a girl born into her class dreamed of owning.

"They told me at the inn that you were sailing," she said breathlessly. "I was afraid I would miss you."

"You nearly did," I told her. I waited for her to catch her breath.

"It may be nothing," she finally said, "but it's something I remembered last night. A name—a man's name."

I guided her out of the path of late-arriving passengers. The ship's bell was announcing readiness to depart.

"A name Lady Hargrave mentioned?" I pressed.

"No, sir," Sarah said. "She had written it on a sheet of stationery I removed from her wastebasket. She had written it over and over again in the manner of an infatuated girl." Her face clouded. "And something else. Above the name she wrote . . . 'My Master.'"

I felt a shiver run the length of my spine and settle at the base of my skull. "His name, Sarah," I said. "What was his name?"

"Aleksandre Denisov," she answered.

I knew the name before she had spoken it. Emile's accusations, I had tried to convince myself, had been the product of a pain-laden mind. Either that, or revenge. But now Sarah was confirming him.

Satisfaction on her face, Sarah asked, "Was it important, sir? Did I do right by coming to you?"

"Yes, Sarah," I said shakily. "You have been a great help."

She beamed. "Then a kindness has been repaid," she

said. Her face lit up with excitement. "I have booked my passage home, thanks to your generosity."

I almost told her the generosity had come from Charles Arledge by proxy, but I held my tongue.

The sailors came to hoist the gangplank.

"*Au revoir, Sarah,*" I bade her.

"*Au revoir,*" she answered in awkward French.

She stood on the dock and waved until the ship was out of port.

The *Capriccio*, in sore need of repairs, was still docked in port when I arrived in Palermo.

I had put many pieces of the mysterious puzzle of Nina into place. Aleksandre Denisov must truly have been her lover—what else would explain her visits to him, her obsession? There had been her attitude the day in the coach when we had witnessed his arrest. Her late-night disappearances from the inn that Sarah had found so baffling. But what of the further implications? What of the suggestions of evil? "My Master"! "Mistress of the Devil"! And Charles telling me, "Where I am wicked, she is evil!"

I remember Nina's saying to me, "Evil, like beauty, may be in the eye of the beholder."

I ask myself many times each hour how Aleksandre Denisov could possibly be her lover. What could she see in the man? How had she met him? And was it true that she carried his child?

Each time I think of these things, I cry, "How could she have done this to me?"

I am aware of sharp, nagging pains within my chest which I recognize as jealousy. I conclude that Nina's attachment to Denisov was born of a loathing of her social position and family. By her own subtle confession, she harbors a resentment of her father. Her involvement with a man of Denisov's class would be a crowning insult to him.

The more I dwell on these things, the more determined I am to find her, to demand explanations—and satisfaction. I feel smothered by my emotions. My hatred grows almost to equal my love.

In Palermo, I sold most of the elegant wardrobe I purchased at Charles's expense, retaining only one costume which I would need to make inquiries at the better inns. What proprietor could be expected to give out information about a guest to a man in the bedraggled attire of the poor? My shoes are in need of repair and my hair could use a trimming, but I can no longer afford these luxuries.

My rounds of the inns, however, have proved unsuccessful. There is no Lady Hargrave registered, no Englishwoman who might be stopping under an assumed name.

I consider the next logical step is to locate the captain of the *Capriccio* and question him. He might have information about his English passenger.

The captain, a bearded man with a pockmarked complexion and sour disposition, informed me he naturally remembered the lady well. He remembered all his passengers, especially those who dined at his table during the voyage. When he informed me there was nothing unusual about her, I knew he was lying. I invited him to join me for a drink at a nearby tavern.

He accepted, but when I again brought up the subject of Lady Hargrave, he drew into himself and became sullen.

I ordered him a second drink and did not press him until he had finished it. Then, "Surely you remember the lady well. She is a great beauty. No one could ignore her or consider her anything but extraordinary."

The captain, leaning forward, folded his hands on the tabletop and looked into my eyes. "The most beautiful woman in the world could have been sitting beside me on this voyage and claimed only a small part of my attention," he told me. "Yes, I remember her. But I remember other things more strongly."

Only my eyes questioned him.

"I knew in Marseille the voyage was cursed," he said. "It was there I saw the rats deserting my ship." He lifted his hairy paw and signaled for another round of drinks. "The sailors saw also. To prevent them from jumping ship, I doubled the night watch and threatened any man who attempted it with hanging from the masthead." His drink was put before him; he lifted the glass and took a great gulp. Wiping his lips with the back of his hand, he went on, "I had to hang the first to prove I was not bluffing. I remember your lady that day. Although I had forbidden it, she came from her cabin and stood on deck to watch. I could swear to you there was a smile on her lips when the rope reached its end and snapped the bastard's neck."

I drained my glass.

"But the lady was overshadowed by her traveling companion."

"Traveling companion?" I blurted.

"The man," the captain said. "Name of Denisov. I swear to you I have never in my life feared any man"—he cast down his eyes and added, "until him. He reeked of malevolence. The sight of him made me cross myself and whisper a prayer to the Almighty." He performed the gesture now as if to ward off the evil that might be summoned by his remembering. "As the fellow moved about the deck, the sailors kept their distances, feeling, I am certain, as I did. He was . . ."

I ceased to listen. I remembered the jailer telling me of Denisov's mysterious disappearance from the prison, a hole cut through the brick wall as if by a flame as intense as a battering ram. I had been too obsessed by Nina herself to give Denisov more than fleeting moments of thought, most of these to curse him should he truly be Nina's lover. The fact that they had traveled to Palermo together was the final bit of information to make my rejection of their affair crumble. My head rang; my senses reeled.

". . . when he looked into your eyes, you saw a glimpse of the torments of the damned." He emptied his glass and pushed it aside, not aware that I had scarcely been listening to him. "The lady was taken by him, that was plain to see. But she had smiled at a hanging." He looked at me questioningly. "Who was she? Who is she, this Lady Hargrave?" he asked. "Who is this man who has the aura of a traveler from the inferno of hell?"

"I can answer for neither of them," I said weakly.

"Have you met the man, her companion?"

"I have," I told him.

"Were you not conscious of the odor of brimstone and sulfur . . . what you would expect to permeate from one who is hellborn?"

I had not been on our single meeting, but I answered, "Yes, I am aware of it now even more strongly than before."

The weather-worn face of the captain lost some of its tension. "Then I did not merely go soft," he said with great relief. "It was not my mind turning to whale blubber." He spoke more to himself than to me.

"Did they disembark here in Palermo?" I asked him.

"Aye. And I was glad to be rid of them," he answered firmly.

"And you have not seen or heard of them since you have been put up in port?"

"Thanks to God, I have not. Pray to God, I shall not." He moistened his lips with the dregs of his drink. "My advice to you would be not to pursue such as they. You seem a decent sort, my friend."

I thanked him, rose and took my leave. What good to explain I could not heed his advice? Nina was a magnetic force drawing me deeper and deeper into my obsession—into, I now feared, an abyss from which there would be no escape.

Tonight I sleep in a room above a fish store. It is scarcely larger than a closet. When I stretch myself out, my head touches one wall, my feet the other. Tomorrow I have enough money for a scant breakfast; then I shall be penniless. If I do not find an odd job, I will be forced to spend my nights huddled in doorways.

Perhaps I can meet a kindhearted whore. I supported them in the past. Perhaps the coin can be turned. God knows, I understand them well enough to appeal to their sympathies.

Or do I?

I am no longer certain of anything.

I have secured the room mentioned in my last entry as a permanent residence. *Permanent!* What a strange word for me to be using. I am the least permanent person I have known. Tomorrow—even tonight—news of Nina may send me away in pursuit.

The owner of this building is a widow—Anna Ferazzi. She operates the fish store below. She is not a particularly attractive woman, with a tendency to plumpness. Her hair is straight and black, and she seldom keeps its combs in place. Her eyes are also black, circled by too much work and little rest. But her heart is good. She has a son, but he is of no account. In the mornings he will not rise to assist her, and at night he has slipped away before his chores are completed. He runs in the streets like an urchin.

The room costs me an hour of my time before sunup and another hour at closing; I set out her baskets of fish, wipe the counters and sweep. Then I am free until closing, when the entire process is to be reversed.

It is a good arrangement, and the widow, because she has not adjusted to the loss of her husband and likes to know there is a man about, cooks my dinner and washes my clothes.

The time between opening and closing the shop is my own. I spend it roaming about the town, questioning shopkeepers and street venders and searching all women's faces for sight of Nina. I have had no results. In my failure to remember which persons I have questioned, I have approached several a second and a third time. I know they whisper about me, saying I am mad.

How wrong are they?

Just before sundown, heavy with defeat, I desert my search and make my way back to the fish store. Even this return trek is not wasted; I continue to search faces and question strangers. Many times I have seen a gesture or expression on a woman's face that reminded me of Nina. My heart quickens; my breath all but stops before my troubled head convinces me the resemblance is minor, maybe even put there by my own longing eyes.

I do not know what I shall do if I do not have news of Nina soon. If she is still in Palermo, I must find her. If convinced she is not, I must think where next to search.

Anna Ferazzi pushed her chair back from the table and heaved a sigh. It had been a long day: profitable, she had told me, but we had closed an hour later than usual. Then she had prepared dinner, pasta and boiled fish, and we had eaten in silence. Now, dinner behind us, she allowed her exhaustion to claim her.

The candles had burned down to their holders, one flickering and smoking in its last moments of life. I sat enjoying my tea: a pleasure Charles had taught me during our friendship; a luxury Anna had added to her household budget for my benefit.

My spirits have become particularly low. My days on Palermo have turned into weeks and the weeks into months. A visit to the docks told me the *Capriccio* had sailed. My obsession with Nina has grown even stronger; it is consuming me. I have lost considerable weight and am listless. I mope about like a man in the final stages of a terminal disease.

Anna was watching me closely with concern mirrored in her dark eyes. She had never questioned me about myself; she had taken me on trust. Now, I felt, she was about to break her silence.

She fingered the stem of her wineglass and said, "I think that it is a woman."

I did not speak.

"A woman who torments you," she continued, determined at last on drawing me out. "Is this not so?"

I considered rising and leaving her, retiring to my room without answering. I stared at the flickering candle as if cuing my answers from the flame. "Yes, a woman," I said in a half-whisper.

"When my Alfonso died I acted much like you," she told me. "I could find no reason for living, no purpose at all." She leaned back in her chair and rested her hands in her lap. "Oh, I got up every day and opened the store. I had done it for so long it was like breathing to me. But I didn't care if I sold fish. I didn't care if they rotted in their barrels. My sense of loss lasted for a long time . . . but it did eventually become less painful. Now, although I continue to think of him each night when I prepare myself for bed, it is with a dull melancholy, not pain." She reached across the table suddenly and touched my hand. "André, you also must conquer the pain."

"Perhaps," I said, "if the woman were dead I could adjust as you have adjusted."

"Can you not convince yourself that she is dead?"

"No! Never!"

She clucked her tongue against her cheek.

What I had said to her kept echoing through my brain: *If the woman were dead! If the woman were dead!* I knew there was no truth to my statement. Even in death Nina Hargrave would haunt me.

I was overcome by such depression that my eyes began to water. I turned my head away to prevent Anna from seeing.

"She must have been a bad woman," she said. "When you came to my door, I told myself, 'There is a handsome man. He will mean trouble for you, Anna Ferazzi.' I thought all the women in the neighborhood would soon be chasing you. And the married ladies, they would say, 'Look at Anna Ferazzi! Her husband's spirit is still earthbound and already she brings a handsome man into his house.' I almost turned you away, but"—she pointed to her head with a heavy finger—"I could see that some woman already had you, had you good. I am but a fishmonger's widow, but I am wise to what is inside a man." She poured herself more wine and sat drinking quietly for a moment. "This woman who drains away your life, is she your wife?"

I told her she was not. Then I added, "I deluded myself into believing she might someday belong to me."

"Why do you search for her?" she asked bluntly.

I had never told her my purpose for being in Palermo. I only stared at her in answer.

"I know you search," she explained. "I have watched you, and people have reported your odd behavior. They say you roam the streets and alleyways and question all those who will not ignore you. They have, of course, started many stories about you. I tell them to tend to their own business, to leave you be, and for that I have been criticized. If I did not run the best fish store in Palermo, they would take their trade elsewhere."

She emptied her wineglass and set it aside.

We did not speak for some time. The candle flame died, and the shadows took on different dimensions. Anna's face appeared almost youthful in the half-light.

"Would it help you to talk about this woman?" she asked. "I know that sometimes after my Alfonso died I longed to discuss him with someone. But that is not always easy. It is difficult to say certain things to friends, people you have grown up with. I sometimes used to sit in front of my mirror like a madwoman and tell my reflection my deepest secrets about Alfonso. It helped, those conversations."

"You are kind to offer yourself as my sounding board, my reflection," I told her, experiencing a warm surge of gratitude. "But I cannot talk of her to anyone."

How would you explain a woman such as Nina Hargrave to someone like Anna Ferazzi, who was simple, loving and limited by her tiny world of home and store? How would she react if I told her the woman who haunted me had used me as an instrument to murder her brother? Had stranded a poor servant girl in a foreign country? Had shot a young man who had confronted her? A woman who was the lover of a Russian mystic whom some called a demon? That she carried this man's child, their bastard? That she was not *good* in any sense of the word? How would I explain that I would search for her as long as there was breath in me?

"No, I cannot speak of her," I repeated.

I detected disappointment in her shadowy eyes. She had hoped to relieve me and at the same time satisfy her own curiosity, but her attempt to draw me out had failed. She smothered her disappointment.

"I am grateful all the same," I told her.

"When you are ready to talk," she said, "I will be your listener." She rose and began to stack the dishes. She carried them to the basin, set them down and then turned to look at me. "Like it was with me," she said, "time will be your best healer."

How mistaken I knew her to be.

A thought that has plagued me all day:

Nina is, in truth, my first love, because this is the only love that has touched my soul.

How horrifying to realize one's soul has been touched by a creature who would send it into hell!

When I came down to breakfast, I was confronted by a sulking Anna. She glanced at me over her shoulder, omitted her usual greeting and turned back to her cooking. At the table, complaining because he had been literally dragged from bed, sat Roberto, her son. I listened to him for a moment, and then told him I had no sympathy for his situation. He, in turn, became as moody as his mother.

When we had been served and Anna had seated herself, she stared at her food and did not eat. Her dark eyes blazed with a fury I had not seen in her; her full mouth was pursed into a near-pout. Roberto opened his mouth between bites to continue his complaining, but was silenced by a look from her. He excused himself grudgingly and went below to tackle the chores from which he had thought himself permanently relieved by me.

"Now," Anna said after he had gone, "you will have the entire day to fritter away looking for your woman."

Her anger was obviously directed at me; yet I did not understand its reason. I pushed my plate aside and reached for my cup. Instead of the usual tea, it contained a strong brew of tree roots which I particularly disliked.

Anna was watching me, expecting me to shove the cup aside. Instead, I drained the contents in one quick gulp, and smiled at her as warmly as any man might at an hour before the sun had risen. This seemed to fan her anger. She rose, carried the dishes to the basin and dropped them into the tub.

I could no longer refrain from questioning her. Last night she had been my friend, a dear friend who had tried to draw me out of my misery with conversation and the offer of an understanding ear. "What is it, Anna?" I asked gently. "What has angered you?"

Her back was to me, and she was supporting herself by

clinging to the edge of the cabinets. Her shoulders suddenly stooped. "You are not even a typical man when it comes to fighting," she mumbled.

"But what have I done that you would fight with me?"

She spun about. "Last night I listened to you," she said. "I watched you when you think of this woman who possesses you, and I start to feel that I want to be this woman. I tell myself it is wrong, my Alfonso only in his grave less than six months, but even so, I want to be wanted, to be alive again." She returned to her chair and seated herself with a weary moan. "But I am The Widow Ferazzi. It is expected that I continue to grieve, that I pretend my body is as dead as my husband's. I thought I had done so." She pointed to her head; "I thought I had convinced myself up here." She shook her head from side to side. "I should never have talked to you, André Laurent. I tried to persuade you that you must fight this passion which drives you, but, Mother of Christ, I succeeded only in awakening myself."

Her frankness caused me to flush. I stared helplessly at my empty cup and said nothing.

"Last night when I went to my room I again became a madwoman. I think that the inside of me will burst into flames and consume me."

"Anna, please," I interrupted.

"No, no! This must be said," she cried. "I cannot have you live under my roof without knowing." She folded her hands, interlacing the fingers, and closed her eyes as she spoke. "I take off my clothes and sit in front of my mirror —the same mirror that only recently listened to my grief— and I tell my reflection about the yearning inside my body. She is a good listener, my reflection. She knows my body intimately; she nods and sympathizes and understands my pain. But there is shame on her face for me: shame because of Alfonso, because of my passion—and because of my envy for this woman of yours. I beg her to forgive me, but she is like an old woman fickle from age. She tells me I must fight my desire, and the easiest way is to turn it into hate. I tell her that it is not you I should hate, but this *woman* of yours. It is the woman who has filled you with this passion, and it is the passion that attracts me."

Anna opened her eyes, but she did not meet my gaze. Instead, she stared at her hands. Although her eyes were averted, I could see that they had brimmed with tears.

"My reflection and I came to an agreement," she finally went on, now in a mere whisper. "It is proper that I should hate this woman, but I should also take measures to protect myself against this power which possesses you."

She rose. Moving back to the basin, she stood with her back to me and stared from the window at the first hint of the sun's rays.

"I decided," she said without turning, "to tell you to leave my house today, but when you came into the room this morning, I knew I could not turn you out. My reflection was wrong. I would suffer as much from worry over you as from my desires."

"No, Anna," I said firmly. "Your reflection was not wrong. I must leave you. I *am* possessed of this woman, and because of it, too many people have already been hurt. I would not want yours added to the faces that now haunt me."

I left her in the kitchen. I collected my things and came away from her house.

It was nearing midnight, and I had not found a place to lodge. Wisps of fog drifted in among the buildings; farther out to sea I could see great banks of it rolling toward the shoreline. I was chilled and hungry and in despair. Thinking I would come across no better shelter, I found the doorway of a warehouse and huddled there.

Footsteps on the cobblestones drew my attention. Unseen in the darkened doorway, I watched a trio of night travelers, a man and two women, emerge from out of the fog and make their way along the street. Coming out of the fog as they did, all three attired in black, they had about them an eerie, unreal quality. If it had not been for their footsteps on the cobblestones, I would have sworn that they floated rather than walked, that I slept and was caught in some nightmarish fantasy.

The trio passed without seeing me and vanished into another bank of fog. I laid my head back on my knees and hoped for sleep. It did not come. My thoughts had not yet settled when the sound of other footsteps brought my head up. Such activity was uncommon so late at night; even if it had been earlier, a night such as this would have kept most people indoors.

The second group to pass me were like the first: all in black, all shadowy forms which appeared to drift into and out of and once again into the fog. I was more attentive now, less concerned with my hunger and coldness. Some-

thing about the appearances of these people reminded me
of Aleksandre Denisov's followers. Rising, I hurried after
them. At first I kept my distance, fearing to be seen, but as
we neared the outskirts of the city, I became conscious
that all about me groups of people moved through the
now dense fog. I relaxed and let myself be guided by
them.

A mile outside the city, the night travelers converged
on a deserted, crumbling château. I lingered about outside
the gates, fearing suddenly to be drawn inside. The silence
was broken by a low, hypnotic chanting from within.
From somewhere within my mind, the thought came to
me, A canticle for the Devil. I visualized Denisov as I had
seen him and drew strength from the memory that his appearance, although not pleasing, had been human. He had
angered and repelled me, but I had not feared him or
thought of him as the master of evil. Still, some inner protective force kept me standing outside the château even
though I knew Nina might well be inside.

A passing gentleman took note of me. He stopped,
peered at me through the fog and said, "Come along inside, my fellow. *He* will not be with us much longer. We
must worship *Him* while we may."

"Is he Aleksandre Denisov?" I asked.

"It's the name he's using," he replied. "But we, of course,
know him as our Master."

If it was as he said that Denisov would be leaving them
soon, then Nina, I was certain, would follow. If all I had
learned of her was true, she would be as much the camp
follower to Denisov as Jacqueline had been to her officer.

The man took my arm, and I let him lead me through

the gate. The courtyard of the château was a shambles. Vines and weeds strangled the walkway and made mounds of fallen masonry. A statue, its face chipped away, leaned precariously atop its fountain pedestal. The château itself appeared near collapse—the roof sagging, the glass gone from all windows. From within flickered the flames of a fire. The chanting grew louder and reached a frenzied pitch.

I held back, suddenly overcome with a fear such as I had seen in the eyes of the captain of the *Capriccio*. It was not a fear one could identify; it clutched at all parts of the body with taloned claws.

The man who led me felt my reluctance to proceed. "Come along quickly," he urged. "Our numbers have grown until there is scarcely room for all of us." He half-pulled me forward. When we reached the veranda, we discovered people spilling into the yard. "It is as I feared," he cried. "There is no room for us inside."

My fear took on new dimensions. These were, however, identifiable. If I did not get inside, how would I locate Nina? If I could not approach her in front of Denisov, I wanted sight of her, if only a fleeting glance.

My companion tugged at my arm. "Come quickly," he said. "We will watch from a window." He hurried about the side of the château with me still in tow.

Our view was limited, but I doubt if my heart would have stood the full spectrum of the scene. I have seen such in paintings and drawings, but always assumed them to be the nightmarish visions of demented artists. In the center of the gutted château, an enormous fire blazed in a pit. About it, some naked and others only wearing the shreds into which they had rendered their clothes, circled a group of impassioned dancers. Their cries were in discord with the chanting of the onlookers who filled every available space along the walls. At one end of the enormous room was an open archway into which the illumination of the flames did not penetrate. Most heads were turned in this direction.

"Is he there?" I asked my companion.

"Yes," he answered.

"Will he speak?"

"Those of us who believe in Him will hear his message within our skulls. He does not need to speak as would a mortal man." He spoke as if I were a novice—not a non-believer, an intruder. "But you shall see Him, my fine fellow. You shall be rewarded. You shall be allowed to glory in the sight of The Master."

My flesh crawled. How could I have ever, even in my ignorance, have considered Denisov a prophet of Christianity? I wanted to flee, but I remained rooted beside the somewhat entranced follower.

"And the master's lady, will she also present herself?" I inquired of him.

"They are all his women," he replied. "He could possess and has possessed them all."

"But was there not a special lady?" I pressed. "I have heard her called his mistress."

"Ah," he exclaimed. "The chosen one!"

I instinctively knew this *was* Nina. "Yes," I stammered. "Will we see her?"

It was a moment before he answered; he was perhaps questioning my reasons for interest in his master's mistress. Finally, he said, "She has been sent away."

The manner in which he said "sent away" made me cry, "Killed!"

He laughed humorlessly. "No, not killed. You are indeed new to us," he remarked. "Even The Master himself would not sacrifice the chosen one. Not before her purpose has been served."

A scream built itself in the depths of my bowels, but my throat became too constricted for it to escape me. All seemed horrifyingly clear. "The chosen one . . . her purpose"! Emile's voice cried inside my head, "She carries his child!"

Turning on my heels, I ran away from the startled devil-worshiper; the frenzied chanting and screams gave my feet a swiftness of flight. But the realization that fled with me could not have been any less hideous.

Nina—my Nina—had been chosen to bear the son of Satan!

I have pulled myself out of an almost cataleptic state to make this entry. The mere writing of my determination will feed it.

I will go to London. I will find and murder Nina Hargrave!

Then I shall be free—and the world shall be spared this horror to come from her womb.

I have secured a position on the docks, loading and unloading the cargo vessels. My employer says I do the work of two men, that I put into my labor what most men save for their off hours. My body has grown strong, my determination to reach England stronger.

Nina must now be in her sixth month of pregnancy. I remember a date she had scrawled on pink stationery, a sheet I had discovered while searching her writing desk for bits of information. That date is in May; she had written above it the astrological sign of Gemini. I had not known its significance then; now I am certain it is the time she expects to give birth.

Is it not ironic that her child will share her own astrological sign?

I hoard my earnings and spend only on what is essential. I sleep in an attic and eat the scraps from the kitchen of a nearby restaurant. My money accumulates slowly—too slowly. I count off the days until I will have saved enough for my pasage. Each night I lie down remembering Sarah and her desperation. My own matches it—no, doubles or triples it! I am driven by an obsession so powerful that all else is nearly blotted from my thoughts.

It has been a month since my last entry.

I have booked passage to Marseille on a French freighter. From there I shall travel by coach to Paris. If I can locate any of my old friends, I will appeal to them for loans to get to London.

If they refuse me, I shall steal what I need from them.

Upon my arrival in Marseille, I went directly to the prison to inquire about Emile. Maybe I could save him.

I was informed that my one-legged friend remained in custody, but I was flatly denied permission to visit.

As I was leaving the prison, I had the good fortune to encounter the jailer I had bribed in the past. He recognized me immediately and spoke to me as if I were a long-lost friend. He had, he told me, boasted of my bravery in entering the cell of cutthroats to every member of the staff. I had become, according to him, a legend. He invited me to join him for a drink, and I accepted.

"Holding my friend," I told him after our drinks had been ordered, "is a grave injustice. After all, the lady did not remain to support her charges."

The jailer agreed with a nod. "But the law is the law," he said, unbending. "The prisoner must serve a one-to-two-year sentence."

"That's absurd! Hasn't he paid enough? If anything, it should be the lady who is in prison. She shot a man, pressed charges and then ran away without supporting them. My friend has lost his leg because of her and . . . !" I almost said because of the neglect of the prison officials, but stopped myself before I made this blunder. "You know," I said, "The English are all quite mad."

"Are you telling me this woman was . . . was insane?" he demanded, and gave me an incredulous look.

"It's a good possibility, isn't it?" I gave him a wink, a smile, and he understood me immediately.

"I see," he said knowingly. "You want me to propose this theory to my superiors."

"Exactly," I said. "I think you should also add that a friend of the prisoner has been collecting information concerning this lady and intends to produce proof of her madness. He might even . . ."

". . . might even cause us an embarrassment," he interrupted with a laugh.

"And will also make it a point to prove the prisoner has been held without cause or proper investigation," I added.

We continued to drink in silence for some time; I refrained from breaking it because I knew a man was more submissive under the influence of several cognacs. He might do for a stranger what he would not even consider for a friend when sober. It was obvious I could not give remuneration in return for his favor.

It was the jailer who broke the silence.

"You are a bad influence on me, Monsieur," he said. "The first time you came to me I was intrigued by you—and a little bit astounded that you should risk your life by entering a cell of criminals to cut off a man's leg." He banged his glass on the tabletop to attract the waitress' attention. "I am also intrigued by your recent proposal. Not that I give a damn about your friend—or even for you, for that matter—but I have been meaning to put my authority with the warden to a test." He ordered our cognacs and lapsed back into silence until they were before us. Lifting his glass to me, he said, "I'll see what I can do."

"Thank you" was all that I could say. I couldn't even pay for the cognac.

"But if I should fail," the jailer added, "it will make me

a very mean man. I'll have to have someone on whom to vent my meanness." He drained his glass in one quick gulp. "I shall then come looking for you. Should I be unable to find you, your friend will know my fury."

I was willing to gamble—and I was certain it was a risk Emile would gladly have taken.

I waited on the knoll outside the prison gate.

It had been a week since my meeting with the jailer, and I had assumed his attempts to secure Emile's release had failed. Then, this morning as I was shaving, a tap on my landlady's door brought her scurrying across the hallway with a uniformed messenger in tow. The young guard closed the door in her face when she lingered to listen to our conversation.

"Monsieur André Laurent?" he asked in a tone that doubted me before I had time to identify myself. "My superior instructed me to inform you that your friend, one Emile Favière, will be released this afternoon."

I stationed myself outside the prison at high noon.

It was a quarter to three when the prison gate swung open and Emile, with the aid of a crutch made of a crooked limb, hobbled from the courtyard and stood blinking into the glare of the sun. I concealed my horror at his appearance: at his unkempt beard, which was flecked by bits of food and crawling things that darted away from the light; at the painful absence of his leg, the pant leg cut off and tied with a string; and mostly at the intensity of his eyes.

He looked at me and said without a greeting, "I understand from the jailer that you are responsible for my release."

I took his arm to assist him onto the path leading down to the streets below, but he shrugged away my assistance.

"I will manage," he said firmly. He moved onto the path, but stopped, dropped his crutch to the ground, and then lowered himself onto the grass. He sat staring at the streets, the houses, the sea beyond—attempting, I supposed, to accept his freedom.

I stood awkwardly beside him, not wishing to intrude upon his thoughts, thinking of him as a stranger. I told myself I should leave him. His fate had plagued me. I had felt responsible, guilty, but now I had repaid him to the best of my ability. What more could he expect of me? I should merely wish him well, walk away and leave him to himself. I cursed myself for having come to the prison to meet him, and I questioned my reasons for doing so. I had deluded myself into thinking I had merely wanted to see for a fact that he was set free, but now I wonder if I had expected some sort of gratitude.

"I was also told that you assisted in the removal of my leg," he said suddenly. Shielding his eyes with his hand, he stared up at me.

"I did what I could," I said weakly.

"You should have let me die." His tone was matter-of-fact. He was not criticizing me—just stating fact. He lowered his hand from his eyes and turned back to the view, staring as a hungry man might at a table laden with delicacies. "You do not appear to have fared very well yourself," he said. "Where are your fine clothes, the effects of a gentleman of quality?"

"Gone," I answered as matter-of-factly as he.

Something came from his throat that resembled a coarse laugh. "You were not real either," he said. "But remember, I did have the foresight to doubt you."

"I remember."

"But I didn't doubt her—your English lady." He repeated the word "lady," and then laughed more openly, more scornfully.

I looked away from him, and said nothing.

"Behind the trappings of a lady lurked the soul of a she-devil," he said, putting more emotion into his voice than he had shown so far. "We became conspirators, your fine lady and I. Were you aware of that, my blind friend?"

I told him that I had come to suspect it.

"She led me to believe I had a chance with her," he went on. "It was not Sarah from whom I was bringing you bits and pieces of information. Everything came directly from her—from Lady Hargrave."

I must have caught my breath, because he lifted his head once again, looked up at me and laughed.

"Oh, I did have conversations with Sarah. I had to know something about the pathetic creature should you question me. But it was the lady herself who devised the allusion to her preoccupation with fortune-telling, her fixation with astrology. She even instructed me to make reference to the tarot cards, but it proved unnecessary. You leaped for the bait like a starving fish."

My throat became constricted. When I opened my

mouth to speak, the words scarcely came out. "But . . . but why?"

"My precise question to her," Emile said. "But she would not answer, not truthfully. She said it was all a joke —a joke on you and her brother!"

"My God!" I sank to the ground beside him. "She knew all along!"

"Whatever it was," he said, "you told her yourself."

I stared at him in bewilderment.

"Your journal," he explained. "One afternoon when you were out of your rooms, she had me let her in with my passkey. I watched for you in the hallway while she read your journal." He turned his eyes to me, cold and truthful, and his lips parted in a mocking smile. "When she came away, she told me it was as she had suspected. She asked me if I would like to be her partner in a practical joke. Her only stipulation was that I not question her. She would explain it all to me later. She also made me promise not to read your journal myself. I did as she asked me."

Trembling, I got to my feet and stepped away from him as if he had suddenly become some venomous creature about to strike out at me. Yet it was not his face swimming before me, but Nina's. Until this moment, I had not truly understood her cunning. I asked myself if her relationship to Denisov could have strengthened her perception—if that was how she became suspicious of me so quickly. Then I remembered Charles saying to me the night I killed him, "We came from the same womb. We understand each other." This was obviously truer than he realized. She had anticipated his actions and had been expecting me, her murderer.

"When I told her the joke—whatever it was—was getting out of hand," Emile was saying, "that I objected to her constantly being in your company and ignoring me, she told me you would soon be gone and I must be patient. She even gave me a rather large sum of money to pacify me." He moistened his lips with his tongue and fell silent.

"And when she shot you?" I asked him. "You did not go to her to plead Sarah's cause, as the simple creature suspected?"

"No, of course not," Emile confessed. "I was on my way to Lady Hargrave's rooms when Sarah found me. The maid had nothing whatsoever to do with the scene between us. I had seen Lady Hargrave leave the inn earlier that day, after you had departed. I followed her to this dungeon"; he motioned with his head to the prison behind us. "I listened outside the jailer's office and heard her pleading for the release of her lover—the release of Aleksandre Denisov, the mystic. She offered them money, sums that would have deafened the greedy, but they remained silent. Thinking this had failed, she threw herself on their mercy, explaining that she carried his child inside her, that unless he was released to marry her she would hang herself on the rafters outside the prison."

He pulled a tuft of grass from the soil and held it to his nostrils to inhale its fragrance. Tossing it aside, he continued, "They were sympathetic to Lady Hargrave, but they explained they were beyond assisting her. Denisov, they told her, had vanished under mysterious circumstances the night before. She baffled all her listeners then by breaking into uncontrolled laughter. It was the laughter of madness. I hear it still on quiet nights."

"Go on," I urged when he fell silent.

"I was going to confront her when Sarah came to me," he told me. "When I did, she admitted everything she had told the guards was true. She admitted it gladly, proudly. She laughed at me for my pain and told me she would be sailing on some Italian vessel. She asked why I should complain—I had been paid." He rubbed the stub of his leg absently. "I cursed her then, but it only made her laugh at me all the more. She told me no man could match her true lover, that he was the master of hell. I thought her demented, but it did not lessen my fury. I made as if to strike her."

He met my eyes again, and there was fear on his face. "At that moment, something most peculiar happened. The room seemed to fill with explosive specks of light, and my ears rang from some mysterious current. When I raised my hand to strike her, it was wedged back against my own face. I was thrown to the floor, almost senseless. Yet I could swear nothing visible had touched me. I was still on the floor beside the bed when I came to myself enough to see her take a pistol from her bureau. Knowing she was going to kill me, I struggled to my feet and tried to flee. She fired the pistol, and the pain that cut through my leg rendered me unconscious."

His brow furrowed. He lowered his head. "You know the rest." Then, lifting his head and staring at me, he asked, "Was what she said true, André? Do you really believe she meant to kill me?"

I told him I had not the slightest doubt of it.

"And you?" Emile asked. "What was the joke she was playing on you? Tell me. I need to laugh."

"I cannot tell you," I told him. "And if I could, you would not laugh, my young friend." I turned and moved a few steps away from him. "But I will avenge you," I promised. "One day soon."

"Will you look for her?" he asked.

I told him I would. "I mean to kill her. As soon as I have the money to travel, I intend to go to London. I will rid myself of her!" I cried out the last part of this statement.

My words continued to echo about me in the cool afternoon air as Emile struggled to his feet and hobbled over to me.

"You are not playing another charade, are you, André?" he asked in earnest.

"Definitely not!"

"Then come with me," he said. "I will finance this venture. I will give you the money you need."

"Where would you . . . ?"

"It's Lady Hargrave's money," he blurted. "The money she paid me for my services! It is only fitting that it be used for the purpose of destroying her!"

PART FOUR

It was late afternoon when I came up the winding driveway and pounded on Lord Arledge's great door. The sun, having fallen behind the surrounding trees, cast long shadows over the lawn—unstilled shadows, because a slight breeze stirred the limbs.

The door was answered by an elderly butler in an immaculate uniform. He lifted his bushy brows at the sight of me and stepped into the open frame as if to protect the house behind him from viewing so ungentlemanly a caller.

I removed my hat and stepped forward as if expecting to be admitted without question. "André Laurent to see Lady Hargrave," I announced.

"This is her father's home, sir," he said.

"I know," I told him. "I also know that Lady Hargrave is residing here."

He closed the door several inches and placed his foot behind it lest I suddenly act the ruffian I appeared. "Lady Hargrave," he informed me coldly, "is not receiving callers."

I stared at him without speaking, adopting an attitude that would tell him I had no intention of being turned away so easily.

"My mistress has been gravely ill since her return from

France," he continued by way of explanation. "Only Lord Arledge, her father, and her doctors are admitted."

"Is she expected to make a remarkable recovery in a matter of some odd four weeks?" I asked pointedly.

His jaw fell open, but he quickly regained his composure.

"As you see," I told him, "I am quite aware of Lady Hargrave's malady."

"What name did you say, sir?"

"André Laurent," I repeated.

He held the door for me to enter. "If you would care to wait in . . . in the study, sir," he said, and motioned me to the proper door.

Inside the book-lined room, I took a leather chair which afforded me a direct view of the closed door. Sitting cross-legged, I steadied myself for Nina's sudden appearance. I told myself she would be changed. She would be swollen and heavy, so close to the time of her childbirth. I knew I must not allow myself to even think about her, that I must concentrate on the dark soul hidden beneath her beauty. If I did not, I would be lost. The ghosts of too many people were counting on me for their revenge—her husband and mother, Charles, Emile—not to mention my own craving for satisfaction. Reaching my hand into my pocket to feel the presence of my pistol, I closed my eyes, and my forehead wrinkled into a frown.

The study door was opened by the butler, but instead of Nina, it was the elderly Lord Arledge who entered. He walked with a cane, his back bent—not so much by age, it seemed, as by some other burden. His white hair had been plastered down across his high forehead. Beneath, his watery blue eyes made a quick survey of the room, failing to locate me at once because the shadows had deepened and the lamp had not been lighted. When he did see me, he gave no form of greeting, but proceeded to the gigantic oak desk near the window and seated himself.

The butler lighted the lamp; then, instead of leaving us, closed the door and stood to one side, his arms folded across his chest. He looked neither at Lord Arledge nor at me, but straight ahead through the many-paned window as if mesmerized by some scene beyond.

Lord Arledge was dwarfed by his high-backed chair and massive desk. He leaned forward, folded his wrinkled hands across the blotter and squinted his eyes in an effort to see me better. "I am told you wish to see my daughter," he said in a raspy voice. He now indeed looked as ill as Charles had once proclaimed him.

I pulled myself up and turned in my chair to face him. "Yes," I told him. "I wish to see Nina."

He visibly flinched at my use of her Christian name. "May I inquire as to your reasons?" he asked.

"They are personal, sir."

"I see," he said with a knowing emphasis. He leaned forward even more until I thought he would leave his seat altogether. "Have we met before?" he asked. "There is something vaguely familiar about your voice—your accent. Come closer! Take this chair." He indicated a chair beside his desk.

Obediently, I switched chairs. Then I was struck by a feeling of uneasiness because the butler was behind me. "If I could see your daughter for but one brief moment," I said. "My business will be quick."

The old gentleman was staring at me intently. "My daughter is seriously ill," he said. His eyes narrowed. "I am told you are aware of the nature of her . . . illness."

"I am," I told him bluntly. "Your daughter is in the last weeks of her pregnancy."

Again, he flinched. "And how do you come to be aware of this, my good man?"

"I know your daughter, sir." Indeed, I thought. I know her as one knows his nightmares.

Lord Arledge pulled himself erect. "Now I remember you!" he cried. "You also knew my son. But your name—it was not then André Laurent. You introduced yourself by another."

I felt something bordering on panic. If the father was capable of putting two and two together, of remembering that it was the night after my visit that his son was killed, then I might find myself in a position I had not taken the time to anticipate. I might stand the chance of being arrested before I had done what I must do.

"Yes, I knew Charles," I told him, ignoring my using a different name on my last meeting. I got to my feet and stood above him. "I must see your daughter, Lord Arledge. I must be allowed to speak with her."

"That, I am afraid, is quite impossible, Monsieur Laurent. My daughter sees no one except her physicians, and them only when I am insistent. She considers her appearance grotesque—which," he added thoughtfully, "is just as well. Being kept hidden from the social world prevents a scandal. At least, for a time." He sighed wearily and stroked his forehead with a long, thin finger. "Please take your chair, Monsieur Laurent. Don't think I shall be intimidated by your youth and strength. Nothing you might say to me would persuade me to let you meet with my daughter." His voice had grown strong, firm. He pulled his hand away from his face and turned to me. The expression in his eyes caused me to drop obediently back into my chair.

"You know about me!" I mumbled in disbelief.

"Yes," he told me flatly, and his face creased with pain. A racking sob escaped his lips, but he quickly controlled himself before others followed. He turned away from me, unable to look into my eyes, and covered the side of his face by propping his hand against it. After a moment, he seemed to regain his composure, if not his strength. He continued sitting with his eyes averted. "My daughter has told me she manipulated you into murdering my son, her brother."

I stammered and then cried out that this could not be true, that he had only surmised as much.

"It is true, so help me God!" he groaned. "She related every sordid detail." He fell back in his chair and sat with his eyes closed. "Does it really surprise you? You say you know my daughter. Do you not think her capable of such an act? What better way to injure me than to tell me herself that she arranged that evil deed? Heartless . . . slut. As I listened to her relating a chain of events so horrible, the telling almost made my heart cease to beat."

Indeed, my own heart was pounding so rapidly I thought it would burst from my chest.

"Upstairs," Lord Arledge went on, "is a woman who is of my own blood, and if it were possible, I would kill her myself. How foolish I always thought my wife to beg forgiveness for their births—both our children. She—God rest her soul and help her forgive—predicted their evil, and I laughed at her. I thought she had taken leave of her senses. She always swore that Nina was the worse of the two, but when I looked into my daughter's soft blue eyes, I saw only her loveliness and not the soul behind."

"Please, Lord Arledge," I pleaded. "You must allow me to see your daughter!"

"No! Never!" he cried. "Do you think I would permit you to do what I would not do myself?" He rose from his chair and walked laboriously to the window. Beyond, it was now twilight, the horizon fading to a brilliant gold. With his back to me, he continued to talk. "I regret that you were caught up in the schemes of my children to destroy each other, but I detest you also for your weakness. You are as despicable as they. I think that they knew more about you than you know of yourself. They knew what was inside you, and they turned it to their purposes." He clutched at the draperies and drew them across the darkening windows with a quick movement of his wrist. "When Nina told me about you, I was in a state of shock for days—no, weeks; but when I eventually had the strength to sort it out in my mind, to consider all possibilities, I knew you would come. I have been expecting you."

He glanced at me, but I did not speak.

"I would have done as much," he said. "Do not deny that you have come to murder her!"

I maintained my silence and considered my fate. It could not have appeared more grim.

"Some men," Lord Arledge went on, "are cursed—or blessed—with a remarkable transparency, Monsieur Laurent. You are one of them. Even Harrington, my butler, read your intentions and mentioned them to me."

Having forgotten the butler entirely, I now turned and saw that he stood with a pistol aimed at the back of my head. The expression in his eyes told me he would have no qualms about killing for his employer. He was only waiting for a signal.

"I considered what I might do when you arrived," Lord Arledge said. "I could, of course, have you arrested for the murder of my son, but I would also be opening this entire matter for public airing." He walked back to his desk and seated himself. "I could have you shot now as a housebreaker. Who's to dispute me? According to my daughter, you are expendable. There is no one who would mourn your death. You are the sort of person who craves involvements but makes certain he becomes involved only with impossible companions. That way, knowing the relationship is doomed from the beginning, you do not have to give anything of yourself. You can merely walk through it with a pretense." His voice fell off as if from exhaustion. He wet his lips and swallowed. "I believe my daughter told me she discerned all of this from reading a journal. I do not remember."

I felt as if the life had been drained from me. I slumped in my chair. "I loved your daughter," I protested weakly. "She was the first. That was real! I did not pretend!"

I heard the floorboards creak behind me and glanced over my shoulder at the butler. I expected to find him approaching to place the barrel of the pistol against my head, but he had merely shifted his weight from one leg to the other.

"Will you have me shot?" I managed to demand of Lord Arledge.

"Not unless you make it necessary," he answered. "Monsieur Laurent, I feel sympathy for you despite myself. You have proved yourself a blundering fool—but perhaps if you had had the good fortune not to meet my son and daughter, you might have learned to live a productive life. Who is to say?" He sighed. "I am going to have you put out of my house. You'll be seen to the gate, and you are not to return. I will have guards placed about the grounds lest you attempt to enter as you did in the past. They will be given instruction to shoot to kill. I could not afford to have you merely wounded and risk the story you might relate to the authorities under examination."

The butler moved forward, his pistol held in readiness, as I rose.

Lord Arledge made no effort to stand. I do not believe the strength to do so remained within him. As I turned to be led away, he spoke hastily. "Do not think I am protecting my daughter for herself," he said. "I have nothing but contempt and loathing for her. But she is pregnant. The child she will bear—your bastard though it may be—will be the heir I have prayed for. My bloodline shall not perish."

My bastard! Then Nina had not told him all. She had spared him the real horror for her own reasons.

"Your prayers were heard in the wrong kingdom," I told Lord Arledge. "It is not my child she carries."

His face flushed. "Whose, then?" he demanded.

"The Devil's!" I said in a shout.

"You are mad!" he yelled, and ordered his butler to remove me without further delay.

I turned at the door and looked back past the butler's shoulder. "You have joined your bloodline to that of hell!" I cried. "Believe me, it is so!"

The butler pushed me through the door.

Around midnight on the second evening of my vigil, the Arledge house blazed with lights. The guards with whom I had been threatened did not take up their positions on the grounds—not unless they moved with the elusiveness of shadows. The gatekeeper's German shepherd barked occasionally, but in playfulness—some game with his owner.

I settled against the trunk of a tree and was still staring up at the house when there was a sudden flurry of activity. There was the sound of horses' hooves on the cobblestones of the carriageway. The gate was drawn open, and a carriage sped through. It turned into the lane and clamored away into the night.

But I had anticipated this sudden flight. I had known from the past, from Charles, that Lord Arledge kept a summer home in Yarmouth. There, I am certain, he reasons he may keep his daughter safely hidden away from me. No vengeful Frenchman, demented as he thought me, would think to look for her in a community that did not come to life until the beginning of summer.

The final rays of the sun were expiring on the roof of the Arledge summer home. There had been little activity throughout the day—the mere comings and goings of servants who had not been prepared for their master's sudden appearance. They scurried about like a nest of excited birds, departing in all directions and returning laden with baskets and bundles of sundry items.

When the sun had fully set and the lights within the house had been lighted, I moved from my hiding place and edged closer. In London, I had approached the door with the intention of brazening it out, but I had not prepared myself for a reception from Lord Arledge and his butler. I had not anticipated being expected. I doubted that the Yarmouth staff had been prewarned of strangers; besides, I had spotted only one male during the course of the day, and he had been old and scarcely capable of getting about. I intended to wait until the household had retired; then I would enter and search for Nina's rooms.

While I waited, I noted a peculiar cast to the sky; although the sun had been down for hours, there was an eerie red glow along the horizon which reminded me of a night during the war when a distant town had been burned and had lit up the night sky. I knew, however, there was no town on the Yarmouth horizon—only the sea and the continent beyond. This strange illumination also appeared to be moving steadily toward the shoreline, toward Yarmouth itself. The air became heavy, static, the night chill being replaced by a heady warmth. The hair on the nape of my neck rose for no accountable reason, and my ears rang with a crackling sound.

No one inside the house appeared to be aware of this phenomenon. Lights were being extinguished as the servants prepared the house for its usual retirement.

Later, when only a single lamp burned in the entryway, I came from the foliage and moved forward to try the door. I had almost reached it when it was suddenly flung open and a young serving girl ran out. She was excited, sobbing; in her haste, she tripped and almost sprawled onto the walkway.

I jumped quickly out of sight and watched until she had disappeared down the slope in the direction of the town.

Lights blazed anew within the house, and the sound of confusion reached me through the windows. I saw an old housekeeper in robe and slippers move from the stairs to the door of the kitchen. When she had gone inside and the door had closed behind her, I stepped forward onto the porch and rapped the knocker. My hand was in my pocket, my finger on the trigger of my pistol.

My summons was answered by a young maid with a flushed face and excited eyes. "You are the doctor!" she cried before I could speak, and grabbing me by the arm, she literally pulled me into the entryway. "Please hurry!" she sobbed. "Follow me!" She was in such a state of emotional upset that she failed to notice I carried no medical case.

She made for the stairs, and I followed.

On the second floor, she led me to a door near the far side of the house. She paused; tapped softly but nervously; then, without waiting to be told to enter, threw the door open and half-pushed me through.

"The doctor," she whimpered, and closed the door behind me.

The bedchamber was lighted by only one dim lamp. It was flickering from the sudden draft from the door. Lord Arledge, in his nightclothes, stood at the foot of a gigantic bed. When he turned and saw me, his eyes flashed with anger and fear, but these expressions were short-lived. He turned away from me as if I did not exist and stared down at the bed.

I followed his gaze to the form on the bed—to the pale and pain-racked face of Lady Nina Hargrave. Moving quickly forward, I hovered above the bed. The beauty I remembered was gone from her. I could see nothing of her as she had been in that face which was drawn by pain, contorted and drained of color.

Still, I reminded myself, this was my Nina—my obsession! I had come to murder her, to end my obsession, to avenge those faces of her victims who haunted my nights. But sight of her did not have the effect I expected. Something unexplainable happened within me. Almost with a discernible snap, my hate and desire for revenge abandoned me. Gone were my memories of the agonies she had caused me, drawn from me with my determination to be the instrument of her destruction. I remembered only those moments of happiness, of love. The recall of them flooded over me, and the emotion became so heavy it brought me to my knees beside her bed.

"Nina," I whispered, but she did not stir.

"In this she will also be the victor," Lord Arledge suddenly groaned. "She is determined to take the child with her into the grave." He clutched at the bed frame, and his head fell down over his chest. "I know this as well as I know myself," he said, his voice cracking with anguish. "She does it as a final display of her evil." He lifted his hand to his face and covered his eyes. "And you!" he cried. "Look how complaisant you are! Do you not care that she tries to murder your child?"

"It is not my child," I murmured.

"Ah, yes," he moaned. "You disown it and call it the son of hell!" He pulled his hand from his face and stared at me, his eyes blazing. "Whoever its father is, it is my grandchild. My blood will pulsate in its veins. It would be my claim to life."

"You do not care for her," I accused him. "Your blood pulsates also in her veins, yet you would give her up gladly for this child she carries." I turned away from him in disgust.

Nina stirred. She drew up her fists and cried out with a sudden seizure of consuming agony.

I drew her hand to me and pressed it between my own, wishing I could draw some of the pain away from her body and into my own.

Nina's eyes fluttered open. She turned her head and stared at me, her vision blurred by her delirium. She blinked rapidly and peered at me, fighting for recognition. "Is it you?" she whispered. "Have you come at last?" Her lips parted in a forced and pitiful smile.

I pressed her hand and mumbled, "It is I, my beloved."

"You!" she shrieked. She made as if to pull away from me, but was too weak to command her body. Her hand remained in mine, moist and burning with fever. "Why did you come?" she demanded. "Do you hope to find delight in my suffering, André Laurent? Or have you found religion and come to plead my case?"

Her struggle for speech pained me. I called her name—"Nina!" Lifting her hands to my lips, I smothered them with kisses, crying, "My beloved!"

"Fool!" she exploded. "If only you might rot in Hell in my place."

"I would do it gladly," I assured her.

"Then you . . . you are more the fool than even I imagined," she cried. Her eyes became glazed once again. She tossed her head back and forth on the pillows. She began to babble incoherently.

"Nina, please, my daughter," Lord Arledge wailed. "Give up the child! Leave something of good to life despite yourself!"

Nina became stilled. She fought to lift her head from the sweat-drenched pillows and glared at her father, a fire blazing in her eyes. "Pray, old man, that I succeed in . . . in sparing you this grandchild. Pray I can return it to where it belongs!"

Knowing of what she spoke, I felt the gooseflesh rise on my arms.

Lord Arledge bent himself to one knee as if he no longer had enough strength to support himself. His anguished, watery eyes met mine. "Plead with her," he begged me. "Make her give up the child!"

I said nothing. How could I explain to him so that he might understand that for whatever reason his daughter had decided to carry her child with her into the grave, it was her greatest gift to him—to all mankind?

"Ah, but even now . . . if he came to me . . . if he proved that I meant something to him . . ." Nina broke off in mid-sentence. Clutching at my arm, she attempted to pull herself to a sitting position, but was forced to settle with her head tilted against the headboard. Her nails dug into the flesh of my arm. Her voice found the power of madness as she bellowed, "*Where is he? Damn him! Damn him for deserting me now!*"

A door opened and closed in the hallway.

Her eyes widened attentively, expectantly. "Has he come?"

"No!" I cried. "No, no, no!"

She screeched dementedly and pushed me away from her. "He must come! He must!"

"He will not," I told her weakly

"Then he shall not have his child!" she cried with determination. "He shall not have it! He shall not!"

She struggled once again as if to rise, but collapsed back onto the bed. It was then that I saw her legs were crossed as tightly as she could manage. She was fighting to trap the demon inside her womb—determined to take it into hell with her, where it belonged!

"The child . . . my grandchild!" Lord Arledge wept.

Nina was seized by renewed fits of pain. Her head tossed on the pillows, her eyes blinking rapidly. Her lips trembled, and perspiration dripped from her face to mat her once beautiful hair against her head. She opened her mouth in what I expected to be another piercing cry of agony, but instead, she mumbled almost incoherently, "I have been nothing to him except an instrument. Pity me, for I have been used as no other woman."

Her body gave a convulsive jerk, and then she lay very still.

I took her hand again and felt for her pulse. Then, turning to Lord Arledge, I told him, "She is dead."

Above his wailing lament, I heard a commotion within the house. It sounded as if the entire structure were being torn asunder. The cries and screams of the servants reached us, and an odor so foul penetrated the room that I was forced to cover my nostrils and hurry to the windows.

Outside, I noted that the red glow I had seen in the sky had reached the house and was enveloping it. All darkness, all colors had faded before the intense redness. The odor grew even stronger, forcing me to struggle with the stubborn latches of the windows.

I had scarcely thrown the windows open to the night air, no cooler or less foul, when the door behind me burst inward, leaving its hinges and crashing into the room.

Even before I turned, I knew whom I would find standing in the doorless frame. I could feel my fear of him crawl over my flesh. He reeked of all things gone to decay. I saw his face—saw it bathed in the glow of redness that engulfed us: a face only vaguely similar to that of the Aleksandre Denisov I had met. It was grotesquely scarred and twisted, with lidless eyes and flesh eaten away from about the cheeks. Truly, his soul was mirrored on his face, and the horror of it will live with me forever. I wanted to hide my eyes, but I could not. I would have flung myself from the window to escape him, but my horror held me rooted to the spot.

I knew why he had come; I knew instinctively that he

had waited until this precise moment when death had claimed the woman on the bed. He had no concern for her. He did not even glance at her face as he crossed to the bed. He had come for one purpose: he had come for his son!

The linen and Nina's gown vanished in a flash of flame, and she lay naked in death, her swollen body scorched and blackened. Yet even in death she appeared to fight him, the muscles of her legs remaining taut.

I prayed to faint and be spared further vision, but I did not. I watched as he uncrossed her legs with apparent ease. He stared for an instant at the heavy mound of her stomach; then touched it almost gently with his gnarled hands. Something resembling a smile crossed and hovered about his lips. Using one taloned finger, he then traced the lump of her belly, and her flesh parted to yield up to him that which she had fought so desperately to carry with her into death.

He lifted the bloody mound of screeching flesh; held it proudly, triumphantly above his head. The air within the room crackled with the static of his demonic pleasure.

This creature of hell had no concern for anyone, anything except his heir. He lowered it to his face and pressed his cracked lips against its bloody mouth as if to feed it with his breath. It became stilled, hushed.

They remained thus for several moments: one horror feeding life and an understanding of evil into the other; father of hell nursing the son of hell.

Then there was a deafening, a blinding flash of light. He clutched his heir against his chest and, laughing victoriously, quit the room as quickly as he had appeared—

leaving Lord Arledge dead upon the floor and Nina, defiled and defeated, upon her bed.

Flames licked at the silk-draped canopy, at the hallway —indeed, at the entire house. The heat scorched my skin, and the smoke, driving away paralyzing horror, gave me scarcely enough power of movement to save myself. I fled the house and ran screaming into the night.

My God! My God . . . !

EPILOGUE

Here the journal broke off.

The authorities, having had it restored, decided to withhold it from the public. Among those who read it, its horrors were debated in whispers—some convinced of its truths and others considering it the demented ramblings of a madman.

But all who read the journal met with disaster.

Some went insane; most were found brutally mutilated.

As for *The Journal of André Laurent*—it vanished and was never heard of again.